Dinosaur Soup: Book One

A Penny For Albert

by Gerri Cook
Illustrated by Chao Yu and Jue Wang

Dinosaur Soup Books

A Penny For Albert

Published in Canada by
Dinosaur Soup Books Ltd.
an imprint of The Books Collective
214-21, 10405 Jasper Avenue
Edmonton AB Canada T5J 3S2
www.dinosaursoup.com

Dinosaur Soup Books and The Books Collective acknowledge the financial support of the Canada Council for the Arts for our publishing programme. We also acknowledge the financial assistance of the Edmonton Arts Council.

Dinosaur Soup Books acknowledges the support of Dinosaur Soup Productions Ltd.

Editors: Timothy J. Anderson and Candas Jane Dorsey
Illustrations & Book design: Chao Yu and Jue Wang
Thanks to Kim Lunquist, Steve Moore, Elan Wang.

ISBN: 1-895836-93-X
Printed and bound by Priority Printing, Edmonton, Alberta, Canada

National Library of Canada Cataloguing in Publication Data

Cook, Gerri, 1948-
  A Penny for Albert

  (Dinosaur soup; bk. 1)
  ISBN 1-895836-93-1

  I. Yu, Chao, 1963- II. Wang, Jue, 1958- III. Title. IV. Series:
Cook, Gerri, 1948- Dinosaur soup: bk. 1.
PS8555.O5625P46 2002   jC813'.6   C2002-910024-0
PZ7.C7697Pe 2002

Dedication and Acknowledgments

This is for my favourite sister Lorraine who was the original Penny even though they no longer share the same interests. I also dedicate this book to my wonderful husband Steve who encouraged me to write this book especially by laughing out loud while reading parts of the manuscript.

Special thanks go to my brother Ray who, as a geologist with an interest in paleontology, is the inspiration for Ben Moonstar. He also proofed the manuscript for glaring scientific errors. My thanks also to Timothy as my patient story editor and to Candas who helped my publisher get the book in print. To Elizabeth for her continued enthusiasm for Albert and Penny, to Alan Brooks and Wendy Sulzle for their development assistance, to Chao and Jue for their great illustrations and to all of those who helped motivate me along the way.

These characters were first created in 1986 B.B.+B. J.P. (Before Barney and Before Jurassic Park) for a potential television series.

—Gerri Cook

Prologue

The Canadian Badlands is the mysterious home of weird mushroom-shaped hoodoos, prickly-pear cactus, scorpions and the prairie rattlesnake. It was once the floor of the vast Bearpaw Sea, over 75 million years ago. Now it is the last resting place for fascinating prehistoric creatures that ruled the earth and her ancient oceans: giant turtles, crocodiles, sea snails called ammonites, and of course, the dinosaurs.

People have been here for only ten thousand years, give or take a few. The Blackfoot Indians still have tipi rings at old campsites overlooking the eerie landscape they called "hills on hills". White settlers crossing this area named it the 'Badlands'. For the First Nations people who live nearby it remains a traditional place to test your courage and discover your destiny.

That is why Joseph Wolf Tail sits cross-legged under the hot sun on his rocky dream bed. He is here on a vision quest in search of a Spirit Guide to help him find direction for his life. For four days he has prayed, without any food or water. When an eagle flies overhead he looks up hopefully, but it doesn't visit with him. He has seen a rattlesnake, a small herd of pronghorn antelope, and a coyote. Each passed him by.

He is weak, hungry and dehydrated. Maybe he should just give up.

Suddenly the earth trembles. What is it? An earthquake? A large shadow falls over him. Joe looks up, and up, and up. His eyes widen, first in amazement, then fright.

An enormous shape seems to waver in the heat waves coming up from the hot earth. It gives a giant roar that reverberates across the Badlands. "Thunder Being!" the young man croaks from a very dry throat.

At a nearby camp, as he prepares for their annual Sundance ceremony, an old medicine man hears the strange roar echoing around the hoodoos. He looks out into the Badlands. His ancient eyes seem to penetrate the distance like a laser. Then he smiles, for his grandson Joseph has discovered his Spirit Guide after all. And it is a mighty one.

Chapter 1

"Three, two, one...you're on the air, Penny!" The red eye of Camera One blinks at me.

I've been doing my *Weird Science Facts* segment on television for most of the school year. I've learned to talk to a camera like it's really a person. So I smile my best eleven- (going on twelve-) year-old smile at the faithful television audience the camera represents, all those Bill Gateses, Grace Hoppers and Julie Payettes of the future.

"Hi! Penny 'For Your Thoughts' Moonstar here, ready for your wildest questions. Give me a call and I'll answer them all!"

It's an experiment. Our Badlands Middle School joined forces with the local cable television station to produce a TV series called *CoolSchool TV*, which is

broadcast every Friday afternoon right after school for an elementary school kid audience. Older students like me create all the programming, run the cameras, switch, direct, write, host, do everything.

The show was the brainchild of our school principal, Ms. Thoth, who is also my science teacher. She's always looking for ways to keep kids busy after school and she sneaks in extra assignments of what she calls "safe learning opportunities". I bet she didn't expect *CoolSchool* would become so popular. Some of our show's hosts even get mobbed by our mini fans at the local mall. It's great when a *Weird Science* fan asks me for my autograph. It's fun to be kind of famous. But it's a responsibility too. Our teachers are always reminding us that the little guys look up to us so we have to watch what we say.

During a break, the floor director hands me some written questions collected from our hard-working phone volunteers. Kids watching the show can call in and ask anything.

Their questions are screened, mostly to get rid of the bad jokes, especially stupid bathroom stuff. Good questions are forwarded to the segment host who tries his or her best to answer them. I get all the science questions. That's the stuff I love. Some day I hope to be a scientific journalist and win a Pulitzer Prize.

" 'Can we save the environment, or is it too late?' " I stare firmly into the camera.

"Hummm. Good question from eight-year-old Kimberly.

"Yes, Kim, we can still save the environment. Start by getting you and your family to clean up around the house. Recycle everything you can, or reuse it. Reduce what you buy. Tell your folks not to put dangerous pesticides on the lawn, and look on the Internet for safer organic products. When you're at the mall, try to buy stuff that doesn't use too much extra packaging. Support good causes. Get your school class to collect bottles and send a donation to the World Wildlife Fund or the Canadian Nature Federation. Don't worry if what you do doesn't seem like a big thing. It all adds up. A little kid can make a difference."

The red light on Camera One winks out. Time to turn to Camera Two for a change of angle and a new question.

" 'How can I get rid of the monsters under my bed?' " I want to smile but I don't. This is a serious question from a scared little kid. "Petey, I have an experiment you can use that might work for monsters under beds. Every night, before turning out the lights, recite some bad poetry out loud. Check with your friends or parents for some great ones or, better yet, make up your own. Good poetry doesn't count. It has to be really, really bad. Like, 'Roses are red, Violets are blue, My feet stink, And so DO YOU!'

"Bad poetry worked for me when I was your age," I tell him. "To those monsters under the bed, it's like hearing you run fingernails down a blackboard!"

Unless you have a tendency to bite your nails like I do. But I don't tell Petey about that.

I check out the next question. "Ahhh, here's a good one. Toni's heard that strange things can suddenly fall on you from out of a clear sky. Is this true?

"Yes, Toni, it's absolutely true." Camera One is blinking again and I nod at it. "There is plenty of historic evidence of this phenomenon. Small fish, frogs, acorns, even rocks, have fallen on people even when there's not a cloud overhead. But no proof that it has ever rained cats or dogs yet. I'll keep you posted, Toni!"

Scottie, our floor director, gives me the cue that my segment is almost over by holding up three fingers, meaning just three minutes left. "Time for one more question from all you fans out there. Humm, here's one from Albert. 'Dear Penny, Are there any other living dinosaurs?' "

I consider the question. "Any other living dinosaurs? I guess you must believe there're still some living dinosaurs around here someplace, Albert. Maybe you're right. There are legends, like the Loch Ness Monster, that could point to dinosaurs. We haven't explored every single remote place in the world...so, who knows, maybe there are some dinosaurs still alive. There are even theories that the dinosaurs really never disappeared in the first place, they just evolved into birds."

Then I just can't resist joking. "There are those who even believe that dinosaurs evolved into certain

teachers, or maybe it was the other way around."
Oops. Now I'm in for it. "But that theory hasn't been
proven...yet!" I add quickly, crossing my fingers.

The floor director is giving me the cut sign,
pretending to slit his throat. "OK, guys, time to go.
Remember that next week I'll be broadcasting live
from deep in the Badlands! So be sure to tune in, 'cause
who knows what might happen! There are lots of
weird things running around in those Badlands...and
next Friday, I'll be one of them!"

"Wow, Penny!" During the break after my segment,
the floor director helps me take off my lapel microphone. "Great show! Especially that teacher crack.
Bet you get into trouble for that one."

"Think so, Scottie?" I smile at him, trying to look
unconcerned. I don't let him know that I am a bit
worried about that dinosaur joke. Scottie is a pretty
cute looking twelve-year-old from grade seven and
this is the first time I've impressed him.

"Are you sure that you can do your next show
from the Badlands?" he asks me for the fifth time.
"There's a lot of fans who'll be real unhappy if you
don't pull it off."

"Oh, sure." I try to conceal my doubts. "No sweat!
My brother Perry tells me he has it all figured out."

"Ha. Ha. No sweat in the Badlands. That's a good
one Penny. Forty degrees Celsius in the shade. No
sweat. You're so funny, Penny."

"Is Penny talking about sweaty stuff again, Scottie

boy?" Twelve going on twenty, Lorrie LaRocque has the segment right after me and she's just slithered up to ruin my moment. Lorrie smiles sweetly at Scottie, showing a row of even white teeth. He smiles back like a total goof.

"If Penny can't make it next week, I can add her time to my spot. My show is much more popular than Penny's 'science for geeks' segment. I always have so many questions from my fans and there's never enough time to answer them all."

I smile back sweetly as I imagine a bunch of frogs suddenly falling out of the sky and hopping around on Lorrie's head. We don't like each other and we don't like each other's shows either. *Love from Lorrie* is where kids write in mushy greetings to friends around town and they gush back. "Bradley, I love your big brown eyes, they remind me of my favourite *Pokemon* character!" and "Sue, do you still have my favourite baseball mitt I lent you last year? Love, Davey"—yuck.

But I am not going to fight with her today. Next week's show will prove that the *Weird Science* segment is way more important than Lorrie's junk mail slot, no matter how popular she thinks she is. "Well, see you live from the Badlands, Scottie," I say as I gather up all my science phenomena reference materials.

"Ah yeah, right, Penny...see yah." Scottie grins at Lorrie like he's lost his last brain cell.

I watch her as she carefully organizes all her red heart and cupid cutouts on the desk so they will show up on camera. "Scottie, could you run and get me some pop?" she asks him, and I swear Lorrie bats her eyelashes—or else some kind of bugs are caught in them.

"Well...I'm not sure...your show is on in five minutes..." Scottie frowns. Going for pop is not in his job description. Lorrie smiles at Scottie again, showing those huge sugar-free chicklet teeth.

"Nice teeth, Lorrie." I can't help commenting when, of course, Scottie rushes off.

"Thanks Penny. They cost my parents a lot but it was worth it to me."

I look at all those teeth and honestly they just remind me of something. "Have you ever heard of a *Crocodilian*, Lorrie?"

"Are you implying that I have teeth like a crocodile?" Lorrie's voice rises as she starts to turn the same colour as her cardboard cupids.

I can't resist. "Prehistoric crocodiles, actually...really neat creatures with great...ah...teeth." I hear her gnashing those teeth as I escape out of the classroom studio.

I rush down the school corridor, late for the bus home. Maybe Lorrie LaRocque won't show those teeth as much from now on and that would be a good thing for the world.

Just then the voice of doom reverberates all around me, bouncing off the metal lockers along the school hall.

"PENNY! Can I speak to you for ONE moment?" Ms. Thoth appears out of nowhere. It's one mystery of science I have never been able to figure out: how Ms. Thoth suddenly pops in front of you as if she's been coiled up inside someone's locker.

"Penny! How many times have I told you that you're dealing with young minds on your show? Things falling from the sky and living dinosaurs are just not scientific. In the future, please stick to answers that are based on reality..." Ms. Thoth frowns "...or I'll have to pull you off the air!"

"Yes, Ms. Thoth." I try to sound contrite. I know that the kind of science I like deals with more than meets the eye. Especially her glittering eye. But now I'm going to be late for my bus home. That is a definite reality.

"Oh Penny, one other thing." Ms. Thoth gives me a hard stare. "Where did you get the idea that dinosaurs evolved into...ahem...teachers?" Ms. Thoth's lips are quivering. Is that a smile? I've never seen her actually make one, so I'm not sure.

"Actually, Ms Thoth, it's my Dad's favorite theory. Sorry, but I have to run or I'll miss my bus." She nods. So I dodge around her to make my escape.

"Your father..." I hear her last comment as I make a run for it. "Oh yes, I remember him very well." It's funny how Ms. Thoth has this way of saying things that always sound like she really means something else.

Chapter 2

The front of our house looks deceptively normal, and from the back we have a great view of the Rocky Mountain foothills. It's when you walk inside that you get a few surprises.

My mom, Meadowlark Moonstar, is an environmental designer who works from home. Her inventions...well let's just say they kind of *grow* on you...actually really grow in almost every room!

Where else would you get to mow the grass in your living room while watching television? Come to think of it, where else do you have a television that's actually set into a rotting tree stump sprouting rare orchids? Or shower behind a curtain made of living green vines? Mom tests these prototypes on us for a few months, then she sells the designs and they get manufactured and sold around the world. She is already famous for her real bluegrass rugs, living cane furniture, and specialty bird telephones.

"Is that you, Penny? Dinner's almost ready." My mother is wrestling with things in the kitchen. It is not her favourite place to be but she tries her best. "Now where did I put the pot roast?" I hear Mom talking to herself as she opens all the cupboards trying to find her casserole dish.

"Look in the fridge, Lark," my father's deep voice booms from his den. Mom calls it Ben's Den, *benzden*, like it's all one word. His private domain reflects his vocation as a geologist. None of Mom's inventions are allowed inside.

His shelves hold books with unpronounceable titles propped up by rock samples, all carefully labeled. Glass cabinets display fish skeleton fossils and ocean shells millions of years old.

Dad is madly trying to finish a report due at the university where he teaches. It's overdue, in fact. He has this ongoing battle meeting modern timelines. He is much more comfortable with keeping rock erosion time. Piled in a heap around his desk are knapsacks, picks, and other geological tools. Dad has planned a three-day expedition to the Badlands for next weekend.

He doesn't know yet that my brother Perry and I intend to go with him.

Mom looks in the fridge for the roast but still no

luck. "I saw the iron in the oven. Maybe they traded places," chimes in my brother, his voice floating up from the basement through the kitchen furnace grate.

She checks the iron cupboard and, sure enough, the pot roast is squatting beside the fabric softener. She whisks the roast into the microwave for a warm-up. She grabs the iron to put it back where it belongs, when she is struck by a new design idea and instantly jots it down on the message board on the fridge. Then she puts the iron in the fridge.

I sigh and shake my head. "Mom, let me help." I get the iron and put it back in the cupboard. It's not that she forgets, really. She gets distracted. Ideas come to Mom so powerfully and neon bright that she just has to write them down immediately.

"Penny!" Dad comes bounding into the kitchen. "How come you're so late? Signing more autographs?" He gives me one of his big bear hugs and swings me around as I protest. Dad rarely ever sees my *Weird Science* segment because it's always over by the time he remembers it's time to turn it on. But he's still very proud of me for doing it.

"Sorry Dad...got held up...by Ms. Thoth." I wheeze after he finally puts me back down on the ground, trying to recover from squeezed ribs.

"The science teacher? I remember her very well." Dad winks at me. "Does she still resemble an old *Edmontosaurus?*"

I finally catch my breath. "She remembers you too, Dad. And she's the principal now." I hear a clatter of little feet running up the stairs.

"Hey, Big P." My little brother Peregrine emerges from the basement. "Your science show was too far out this time."

Perry is eight and a typical younger brother. If you have one, you know what I mean. He loves computers, inventing things, and bugs. Real bugs. He also likes to watch my show so he can criticize it.

"Now, Perry," Dad says as we sit down for dinner, "you know your big sister's theories are usually *rock solid*...rock solid, like that one?" We groan.

Mom joins in. "There's nothing wrong with a creative approach too." She adds sweetly. "Never let pure science *bog* you down!"

"Humm," responds Dad, his eyes gleaming. "But it's also important not to take things *for granite* either, wouldn't you all agree?" Dad helps himself to a large serving of organic mashed potatoes in triumph.

Dad loves puns, especially bad ones. He considers himself the champion punster in our family. Mom gives him some competition when her mind isn't on her latest creation.

Mom brings the roast from the microwave to the table and sits down, shoving one of the vines from her living cane chair out of the butter. She looks around. "Has anyone seen the bread?"

"Try the bathtub," I suggest.

Mom stares at me, astonished.

"I noticed a trail of crumbs," I tell her.

Perry runs to check out my bathtub theory. "Found it!"
He brings the bread back to the table like the winner
of a scavenger hunt.

Just then our imitation snowy owl phone starts to
hoot. Mom sighs. "Penny could you please get that? I
forgot to leave the answering machine on. Let whoever
is calling know that we're in the middle of dinner
and we'll get back to them."

"Moonstar residence," I answer.

A man's voice with some kind of accent rasps,
"Could I speak to a Penny Moonstar please?"

"Speaking." Something about his voice skitters up
the back of my neck.

"Ms. Moonstar of *Weird Science?*"

"Yes. Can I help you?"

He sounds strange. "We are enquiring into the
whereabouts of the caller who asked you if there are
any other living dinosaurs, during your television
program this afternoon?"

"Hummm. I'm sorry, I'm not allowed to reveal
that information." Maybe this is just a kid playing a
practical joke, trying to disguise his voice, but I try to
be polite just in case the call is for real.

"All I can tell you is his name was Albert. I don't
think he left a number or anything." There. That
couldn't hurt anyone, could it?

"I see," he says, but I can tell he thinks I'm being difficult. "Let me give you a number to call, in case this Albert ever contacts you again. I'll make it worth the trouble." He gives me a number that is definitely long distance. Then he hangs up.

"Who was it, Penny?" Mom asks as I head back to the dinner table.

"Just a fan." At least that's what I hope he was. The hairs on my neck are still quivering.

"Guess what, electronic family unit! I've adapted my computer search program." Perry announces. "Now I can interface with some really wild stuff from outside the country. Who wants to see?"

"Define what you mean by 'wild stuff', son," Dad says sternly.

Perry looks at all of us impatiently. "Wild animals on camera, natch! Now I can tune into all the remote animal webcams set up around the world.... 'Course there are a few glitches to work out."

"All your inventions have glitches," I point out.

Perry frowns. "Hey, whad' you expect, Big P? I'm still a kid. Do you wanna see what I got or not?"

"Just no more power outages, OK?" Ben pins Perry to his chair with a very firm look. "I lost my entire paper on ammonites last time, a week's worth of work. One minute, it was there, and the next just a blank...*slate.*"

"Ahhh, Dad." Perry winces at Dad's latest pun. "I'm being careful, I promise. Besides, it was really Penny's fault. I told her not to plug anything in."

Perry is trying his patented 'divert the blame' routine and so I deflect it with the 'outraged victim' counter response. "*My* fault! How'd I know that when I tried to plug in Mom's curling iron, the lights would blow out for the whole block!" Then just as I'm winning the argument, Perry wiggles his ears at us. He knows how much I hate that, especially since I can't do it. Dad tries to hide a smile.

"Perry, I'm serious. If you don't want to be *grounded* in the near future, you'd better keep what I said in mind."

Mom can't resist. "So remember, no more *shocks*, son."

"Arggg." Pleading for mercy, we flee down to the basement before our parents come up with more *bright* puns.

Chapter 3

Perry's Cave is a computer geek's dream. There are strange things hooked up to his computer to upgrade, enhance and otherwise increase his ability for game playing and Internet surfing.

The rest of the basement has been converted too, crammed with things started and never finished. He has pictures of some of his favourite inventors: Nikola Tesla, Leonardo da Vinci, George Washington Carver, Reginald Aubrey Fessenden (the inventor of radio), and Grace Hopper (the computer pioneer who coined the phrase 'computer bugs').

What's really neat is that he has also inserted a sketch or photo of each inventor when he or she was around his age—for motivation. Perry is ambitious.

The rest of his posters include a mix of robots from fiction and the movies, award-winning machines from *Rock Bots*, one of his favourite TV shows, and close-ups of big insects. Perry always wanted his own Stickbug but Mom's plant furniture and the grass carpet would be too much of a temptation for pet bugs who might get loose. Only electric bugs and ancient fossils are allowed in the Moonstar home.

"OK, Peregrine, show me your latest!" I tell him.

"Coming at you, Pentacrinus!" he zings back.

I wince. Pentacrinus, Penny for short. Wasn't it just my luck that I have a father who would name his only daughter after a sea lily fossil from the early Jurassic Period, 180 million years old?

"OK, Perry," I tell him. "Just be sure you never tell anyone what Penny is short for and I'll lay off the Peregrine." He was named by our bird-loving mother.

Perry nods and we shake on it.

Punching up his computer, Perry is soon playing tour guide around the world via cameras set up at watering holes and outside animal dens. At first it's like watching paint dry until we see something move.

"Look, it's a rare Kermode bear," he tells me. "A lot of these animals are on the endangered species list, Penny."

"Neat!" We both watch as a pure white bear from the Pacific Coast catches and munches on salmon in a clear, foaming stream. Kermodes are not polar bears but black bears that are cream-coloured. Perry tells me they are called *Spirit Bears* by the west coast Indians.

"Who's paying for all these web-cameras?" I'm amazed at how many different sites there are.

"Some rich guy who must really care about rare and unusual animals." Perry shows me the home webpage. "See...here it is...brought to you by the initials T.T. I'll show you his logo. It's great: a rare giant Amazon tarantula!"

A big hairy spider scuttles across the screen dragging the T.T. initials behind it. "I wonder what those initials stand for?" I ask feeling my skin start to crawl. I can't say that I like spiders, especially huge ones, even though as a future scientific journalist I know I have to get used to them. Someday. But not now.

Perry shrugs. "Don't know, but this T.T. must be a good guy cause he's set up these web-cams to watch over the rarest and most endangered animals in the world!"

Suddenly, Perry's computer monitor goes black and then a flood of flashing warning signs and error messages erupts with graphics of what seems like a zillion spiders trapping the word 'Trespasser' in webs.

"Perry, are you sure that you will be able to do a live remote from the Badlands with this equipment? I could lose my show if we don't pull it off." I shudder, thinking of Lorrie LaRoque and all those white cuspids and red cupids invading my show.

"No problem, Big P., I've got it all figured out," my little brother says confidently. But all that's now showing up on his screen is that ugly big spider jumping up and down and the phrase 'Unauthorized Entry' flashing over and over again. Then the computer crashes.

Chapter 4

In my opinion, our doorbell is one of Mom's most successful inventions. It rotates through twelve different songbirds. This time, it warbles the first notes of a redwing blackbird's call.

I open the door and I can't help staring at the visitor: Ms. Thoth! She stares back, waiting for me to ask her to come inside. Ms. Thoth has never made a house call before, I am sure of it. She's standing there, her purse held waist-high in front of her middle, and I notice how small and claw-like her hands are. She really is like a dinosaur.

"Hello Penny. Are your father and mother home?"

"Huh, just my Dad." My face feels all hot and I hope she can't read minds. Why does she want to see my parents? Does she know Perry and I plan to skip school on Friday so we can go to the Badlands with Dad?

"May I come in?" Ms. Thoth's voice is chilly, and that means trouble.

I lead her into the living room. I can see her eyeing all of Mom's inventions. She carefully sits down on our couch and avoids having her feet touch the bluegrass carpet. Ms. Toth is rumoured to have an extensive collection of exotic lizards and bugs in her home. Perry says she even has a collection of pet spiders. No wonder nobody likes her.

"Ms. Thoth, would you like any refreshments?" Maybe if I'm extra polite she won't tell my Dad I called her a dinosaur. Or maybe she's cancelling my show, and she wants to tell me in front of my parents.

"Perhaps some tea."

Of course. Tea. I nod and then run to get Dad, who heard the doorbell and is already on his way. We almost run smack into each other in the doorway of the livingroom.

"Bertha Thoth?" He stares at her. "Is that really you?"

Ms. Thoth stands up and shakes my Dad's big hand. "It's good to see you again, Bentonite. You look just the same—well, perhaps a bit older."

Dad hates to have anyone use his whole first name too. He was adopted when he was little by a geologist who called him after one of his rock discoveries.

Dad probably called me Pentacrinus so he wouldn't have the weirdest name in our family.

I jump in: "Caffeine or herbal?" Dad and Ms Thoth stare at me. "Tea. I'm making tea."

"A good idea, Penny. Herbal, I think." Dad says. "Now, Ms. Thoth, what can we do for you?"

On the way to the kitchen I can barely hear Ms. Thoth who replies in a voice much softer than the one she uses at school. "Well, Ben, I received a disturbing call at the school today..." Then she lowers her voice and I can't hear anymore.

As soon as the tea is ready, I carry it in. Dad now looks very serious. Ms. Thoth is standing up, about to leave. "Tea?" I remind them. Ms Thoth looks at me. "No thank you, Penny. Perhaps another time. I've said what I had to say. By the way, your father tells me that you and Peregrine would like to take a trip with him to the Badlands but you'd have to miss school on Friday. Under the circumstances, I think it's a good idea. You both have my permission to go."

With that, she marches firmly to the front door. Just before she leaves, she turns around and says "Tell your Mother that I like the redwing blackbird door bell." Then she's gone, the door closing behind her with a precise snick.

The sound of a motorcycle squealing off down the street makes me open the door again, but I can't see Ms. Thoth or a motorcycle. I don't think of Ms.

Thoth as the kind of teacher who would ride a motorcycle. In fact such a crazy idea makes me smile.

Dad carefully picks up one of the hand-decorated ostrich egg tea cups made by Mom and takes a sip of tea. I want to know what Ms. Thoth said to him and at the same time I don't want to know.

"It's not you, Penny," Dad says, and I get the feeling he knows what I am thinking. "It's Perry. Apparently he broke into an unauthorized website a number of times this week using a school computer and there's been a complaint. It could be very serious. Hacking is against the law."

That blasted hairy tarantula flashes before my eyes.

It's a good thing Perry is only eight. In the end, Perry has to promise he will never go into the T.T. website again. He also has to write a letter of apology and e-mail it to the corporation in London, England, that owns the site. That's where my Mom's only sister and my cousin Derek live. I've never been to England. And now knowing that there's some mean corporation headquarters that reported my little brother to the computer police, I'm not anxious to visit there either. T.T. probably stands for *Terrible Temper or Too Touchy*, I tell myself. But at least Perry isn't grounded and we have permission to take off a day from school to go to the Badlands with Dad. I can't wait for Friday.

Chapter 5

By Friday morning, Perry and I are on our way into the Badlands, bouncing along in Dad's heavy-duty four-wheel-drive truck.

"Get your elbow out of my ribs, Perry." The cab of the truck is crowded with all his computer equipment and other mysterious things Perry insisted on bringing along. I also have my trusty knapsack, stuffed with various odds and ends that might come in handy. Dad's tools are in the back of the truck, along with our camping gear and dry staples, but Mom packed us a basket with some snacks to keep us going on the long drive.

"When's lunch?" Perry asks. "I'm hungry."

Dad negotiates carefully along the narrow side

road that takes us into fossil country, then turns off the road and—using his four-wheel-drive—takes us down into a coulee with a bit of vegetation and shade. "I'd like to check out some likely-looking ammonite formations around here. Let's have a bit of lunch then do some exploring. If the area looks good, we might even camp here for the night."

He pulls over and we get out of the cab. I've been keeping an eye on my watch. My *CoolSchool* segment starts at 4:15 p.m. and Perry has to get everything set up for our first-ever remote feed. We still have plenty of time.

"Come on, kids," Dad says to us as he brushes off the top of a small hoodoo and puts the basket on top. A hoodoo is a tower of soft sandstone that has been topped by a slab of harder rock so that it erodes into a spooky shape like an animal or person standing tall, but with a hard flat head. They come in all sizes and are part of what makes the Badlands so interesting. Dad has seen so many that they're like old friends to him.

The first things out of the picnic basket are three carefully folded white towels, too large and fuzzy for napkins. Then comes one of Dad's shirts, some socks, and my clean coveralls. Oh no. Mom has exchanged the laundry basket for our lunch.

"Wait..." says a desperate Perry as he digs down towards the bottom, "I see something!" and he pulls up one large can of pork and beans.

When you're hungry and sitting in the middle of nowhere, cold pork and beans are surprisingly good. At least they take the edge off.

"OK, kids. Now I'm going to check out some formations just over there." Dad carefully wipes off his mouth with one of the clean towels. "What are you two planning to do?"

"I've got to get my computer set up. I have to orient it to one of the communications satellites so that I can set up a remote for Penny's show."

Dad is impressed. "You have enough power for that?"

Perry is evasive. "Uh, sure, Dad....I have it figured out."

"That's my boy. And you, Penny?"

"Well, Dad," I say, "I want to do a bit of exploring while Perry gets set up. I have to find things to talk about for my segment."

"Now be careful, you two. There are black widow spiders, prickly pear, and—"

"We know, Dad," we both chime in unison, "—rattlesnakes."

Dad smiles at us before heading off to look for prehistoric goodies in the nearby sandstone rocks.

I pull out my notepad and pencil and zip up my trusty knapsack. "OK, Perry. I'll go check things out, and be back in about an hour or so. Will everything be ready in time?"

Perry is pulling out cables and other stuff, including a hand-held device he traded from somewhere that will let him link with the Global Positioning Satellite, or GPS as he calls it.

"I'll be ready. No sweat." Perry sounds confident but I am beginning to sweat as I start out exploring the Badlands. I really want this show to work. If it doesn't, then Lorrie LaRocque and her cupid cuspids will be chomping up my only air time.

If I could just find the scoop of a lifetime, then I would never have to worry about *Love From Lorrie* again.

Chapter 6

Everything is going fine until I detour to avoid a big prairie rattlesnake sunning itself on a rock. That's when I notice the giant chicken tracks, way bigger than my own feet, heading into the coulees.

My first thought is that Perry is playing a trick on me. Or maybe my Dad and Perry made these footprints and they're waiting right around the next hoodoo laughing their heads off. But that doesn't make sense. We were all together at the campsite and both of them were totally into their own thing when I left to start exploring.

Maybe it is the trail of an ostrich, a very big ostrich. There are ostrich ranches in the area—maybe a bird has escaped. This could be the scoop I need for my show, so I follow the tracks.

It isn't easy to follow three-toed footprints through the dusty, pebbly coulees with the sand flies bugging you and a heavy knapsack making you feel like your knees are made of melting rubber. Then I hit harder ground and the tracks disappear.

I keep looking, my eyes glued to the ground as I go around cracks in the stony hills, trying not to lose sight of the faint scratches that might be tracks or might just be where the wind blew a twig over the sandy path. So that basically is how I get lost.

Now being lost in the Badlands is not a good idea. Plus I have a live show to do in a few hours or lose my slot to Lorrie and spend the rest of my year dissecting worms for my science assignments. I look for a good spot where there is a bit of shade. There I open up my knapsack—it's a good thing I remembered to take my knapsack—to sort through my emergency kit.

I don't have a cell phone, because Mom and Dad are afraid the waves will hurt my brain. But I find a small battery-operated fan. This is a good start because I need to cool down. Next, I find my mini-recorder for dictating notes. I decide that I might as well record my final words before they find me, a dried up mummy with messy hair, lost in the Badlands.

"HELP!" I yell. My voice echoes off the hoodoos.

"Get a grip, Penny," I tell myself. Time to take Dad's advice on what to do if you think you're lost: don't panic.

"Testing. Testing. Penny Moonstar here, live in the Badlands...I hope." Good, the recorder is working and the fan is cooling me down. Time to check out the landscape, look for features that might help me retrace my steps.

They say when you're lost you should stay where you are, so people can find you. Should I stay or leave? I check the time. Still a couple of hours before the show; plenty of time to find my way back. Relax, breathe deeply, and think calm thoughts. Soon my thoughts become so calm that I fall asleep in the shade of a friendly hoodoo.

The heat and lack of anything to eat except cold pork and beans along with the soft whirring of my trusty little fan must have put me under. It's the ground bouncing up and down that jerks me awake.

I'm lying on my back with my eyes squeezed shut as the earth shakes under me. It's an earthquake. Soon I'm going to fall down a crack and never be found again. Lorrie will get my show and no one will care except my family.

Boom. Boom. Shake. Boom. Boom. Shake.

Wait. This trembling is too rhythmic for an earthquake. I cover my eyes with one hand, cautiously open them, and then peek through a space between my fingers.

The light here in the Badlands plays tricks. I think I can see two huge three-toed feet with long talons that can use a trim. I look further up, squinting a bit because of the light coming from behind the creature. Two large muscular legs. A big stomach. Is that a tail? Two small arms. A long neck. A big head. And...a nasty, big set of teeth the size of a prehistoric shark's leaning over and grinning at me. I must be dreaming, but just in case I'm not, I point the only weapon I have: my mini-fan.

"Take one more step and you're chopped liver!" One big foot hesitates over my head. Then my fan conks out. The battery is dead. And so am I.

I close my eyes.

I feel one of its toes hook my knapsack and I'm lifted into the air. I open my eyes. I'm dangling about twelve feet off the ground! A big yellow eye stares at me. It's a dinosaur eye. I've seen all the *Jurassic Park* movies so I know what comes next. I prepare to battle to the death and I scream. It's a good piercing one with plenty of lung power.

The monster drops me.

I sit up and look around. Everything is quiet. No monster and my fan is working again.

"What a nightmare," I tell myself. "That's the problem with having too much imagination!" I dust myself off.

My recorder is lying on the ground, still taping. I pick it up, rewind for a second, and press the play button to hear the last sounds it caught. There's my scream.

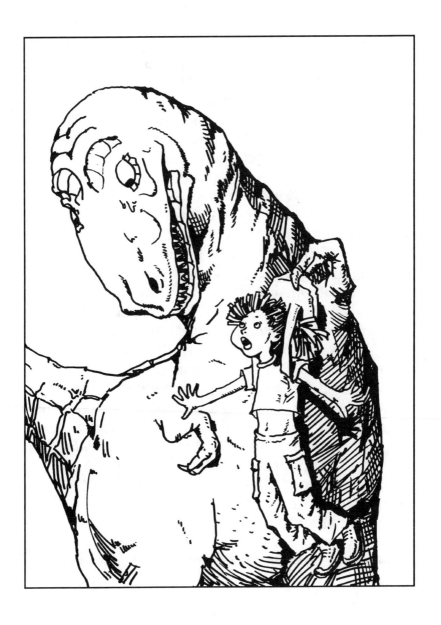

"Too many *Jurassic Park* movie sequels," I tell myself, rewinding my tape further back. There it is on the recorder. Boom. Boom. Shake. Boom. Boom. Shake. Silence. And my scream.

Then I see it again. Peeking cautiously around the hoodoo. It looks like a big, live dinosaur. I pinch myself. "Ouch." I'm definitely awake.

Then all of a sudden it speaks.

"Are you OK, kid?"

"Uh. Uh." I don't know if it works the same way with dinosaurs as with people, but the low voice makes me think this one is a he, and now he's back towering over me.

"Almost stepped on you. Sorry. But I didn't expect any more Spirit Guides to be lying around out here."

I am still staring when he gives a big shark-toothed grin. "Allow me to introduce myself. The name's Albert O. Saurus. But you can call me Albert."

He leans down to give me a friendly handshake with one of his small front arms which are about the size of my own. Even as I extend my hand and shake, I can't believe I'm doing this. I am meeting a *dinosaur* in the Badlands. It speaks English. It's talking to *me*.

I'm...ah...Penny... ah...a reporter for *CoolSchool TV*," I manage to choke out.

"Penny Moonstar from the *Weird Science* show?" Albert is bouncing excitedly around me, which is a pretty serious situation since he must weigh over a tonne.

"You've heard of me?"

"Of course!" He continues to bound up and down. I'm feeling seasick as the ground shakes under me. "Your channel is the only one I can pick up out here! I sent in a question—the one about whether I was the only dinosaur left?"

"Albert." I feel like I'm about to throw up. He finally stops hopping around and examines me with his other yellow eye.

"Penny, you look a little green—which is one of my favourite colours, I might add. Sorry about that. I still have trouble dealing with you puny humans. It's bad enough dealing with all the other changes around here. I don't recognize anything anymore."

"Wow!" I walk around him. "I can't believe it! A dinosaur! A real, live dinosaur!" I poke him, to make sure he's not really some kind of big puppet, and he giggles.

I look up at him nervously. "Oh, sorry."

He leans over and pats me on the head in a friendly, I think, fashion. "It's OK. I'm extremely ticklish and I wouldn't want to accidentally squash you." I gulp and nod in agreement, careful to keep my hands to myself.

"Did that to a young friend of mine once. He never trusted me after that." Albert looks off towards the horizon again. "He was one of those flat-lipped weed-eaters who liked to hang around in the water."

"You squashed a duck-billed dinosaur?"

Albert quickly swings his big head in my direction. "Course I didn't squash him. He's a lot bigger than you are...or he was... I just bruised him a bit playing a great game of swamp tag."

"Swamp tag?" I am starting to feel like a parrot.

"Yes. I wasn't supposed to be friends with him. Eat him, yes, but best friends, no. Mother was always after me not to play with my food." Then Albert looks sad again. "Poor old Mom. I wonder where she is now...."

To my great dismay, Albert sniffs, then a big tear rolls down his face, a tear the size of half a pint of water. This is a dinosaur who could use a little cheering up.

"Look I'm sorry about the duckbill and your Mom, but Albert! Don't you get it? This is mega amazing! You're a dinosaur, alive in the Badlands!" I dig around in my knapsack for my voice recorder.

"True," says Albert nodding.

"And I've got the scoop! I can win the Pulitzer Prize for this! I see it now: Penny Moonstar, greatest scientific journalist for her age in the world!"

Albert sighs "Uh, kid. Don't mind me, but I haven't got another million years, you know."

I hold up the recorder as high as I can to get every word of this exclusive report. "I'm interviewing Albert O. Saurus, the world's only living dinosaur—"

"Ahem...that's me." Albert smiles.

"Now, dinosaurs are supposed to be extinct, finished, done for, wiped out, dust, old bones, you know, goners for millions of years!" I continue.

"Take it easy on the overkill, kid." Albert looks a bit pale.

"Uh, sorry, Albert." I don't want him to burst into tears again. Buckets of dinosaur saline can't be good for tape recorders. "So, how come you're still alive? Where did you come from? What happened to all the rest of the dinosaurs? And how do you know so much, like how to speak English?"

I hear a very loud rumbling and look around. A thunderstorm? Albert pats his stomach. "Oops, sorry, Penny. I'm hungry. Time for my afternoon snack."

Suddenly I realize that, unless I'm still dreaming, I'm actually having a conversation with a young *Albertosaurus*, who stands around three metres—or ten feet—tall at the hip, and is one of the biggest meat eaters to ever live. And he's alive.   And hungry.

"Uh...hum...what do...ah...what do you like to...er..." I am afraid to ask.

"Eat? A lot! And it isn't easy finding enough food around here," Albert responds, rubbing his loud, growling stomach and staring at me. "Say, how much do you weigh, Penny?"

I wonder if I can outrun him. "About thirty-two kilos. That's about seventy pounds, mostly bone and muscle. See?" I flex my arm and suck in my cheeks. "Very stringy."

Albert looks me over carefully. "You need to fatten up! Let's go to my cave. It's nearby. I'll whip us up something to munch while I tell you the story of my life."

He lumbers off and I follow, wondering if I'm making a big mistake. Maybe I am his next snack. But I need this story. I still have over an hour left to get back to my brother and go on the air with the story of a lifetime.

"Oh, and Penny," Albert turns his head to look down at me, "just one thing. What's a duckbill dinosaur?"

Chapter 7

The entrance to Albert's cave is hard to see unless you know it's there. It looks like a shadow in a sandstone cliff, but inside it is big, with sparkling stalagmites and stalactites hanging down or coming up out of the floor. The next thing I notice is that this is someone's home. It has at least two natural skylights where there are cracks in the ceiling which provide a nice diffuse light.

"Let me give you the grand tour." Albert leads me around proudly. "Those are my rock shelves." He points at a row of sandstone slabs stacked at least three metres tall. "They hold my books, videos and CDs. I've just started on my collection. It's hard to get home delivery out here so Joe brings things when he visits."

"Now over here is the kitchen. It's big because I love to cook." I look in amazement at what appears to be a working stove carved out of rock. "It's powered by electricity." Albert tells me. "Neat stuff when it's harnessed. It just used to cause fires back in the good old days when it was only lightning."

"But how do you get electricity 'way out here?" I stammer.

"Simple," Albert replies. "A generator powered by my hot pool over there."

He leads me into the back of the cave past a number of intriguing nooks and crannies, to where a hot pool steams and bubbles. It seems to be running a small electric generator. Albert explains. "Of course Joe helped me with all this. Don't know what I'd have done without him. Live like an old-fashioned dinosaur, I guess. Now I even have a television, and it gets one channel. That's how I watch your *Weird Science* show!"

"Who's Joe?" I ask, looking around amazed.

"The first human I saw after I woke up. At first I didn't know what he was. There were none of your kind when we ruled the swamps. But now I'm his Thunder Being and he's my Spirit Guide." Albert moves over to the stove.

"Thunder Being. Spirit Guide. Right." This is all very strange.

"Hope you like spaghetti with meat sauce. That's

Joe's favourite." Albert puts on a chef's hat which perches on top of his big head. At the stove is the biggest pot I have ever seen. He sees me looking at it.

"This pot is a bit small, but good for whipping up leftovers for an afternoon snack."

The cold pork and beans for lunch are now a distant memory. "I love spaghetti," I tell him. "Can I help?"

"Oh no. Everything is just about done. I make a pretty tasty pasta, if I do say so myself. Usually I sing when I cook. Do you like opera?"

"It's...OK," I tell him. I'm not about to tell an *Albertosaurus* opera fan that to me opera resembles two large football teams bashing and yelling at each other in a foreign language until most of the players fall down dead on the field. Whoever's left standing is crying. Nobody ever seems to win.

"Do you know this one?" Albert starts humming something. "It's *Il Trovatore*, about a jealous Count, which I think is something like a King meat-eater, who wants to kill his brother because they're in love with the same lady."

"That's not very nice," I comment.

"Oh, the Count doesn't know it's really his brother because his brother was supposed to have been thrown in a fire by a gypsy when he was a baby. The gypsy is really the daughter of a witch who was burned in the fire by order of the Count's father.

"So she steals the old Count's baby son and throws her own baby into the fire. Then she raises the old Count's baby as her son. She is going to get her revenge by telling the Count that he's killed his own brother after it's too late. Oh, and the lady they both love kills herself afterwards I think. It's a really famous opera."

I shake my head. "That's a terrible story," I tell Albert.

"Right," he nods happily. "That's why they call it a tragedy. Everyone dies at the end."

And people worry about violence on television and video games, I think to myself. Has anyone ever checked out these operas?

Albert's voice is a deep bass and rumbles around the cave. Some of the rocks vibrate when he hums, which makes me nervous. Albert takes out two huge bowls.

He puts most of the spaghetti in my bowl with a dab of lumpy-looking meat sauce. Then he pours the rest of the meat sauce into his bowl over a few strands of pasta.

"Here you go. Most of the pasta is for you because I prefer just meat sauce myself."

I wonder what a meat-eating dinosaur would put into his own sauce, but suddenly I'm temporarily deafened by a rhythmic, tuneful roar. Albert is now singing—loud—in Italian! At least, it sounds Italian, like my friend Paolo's family when they are talking to each other at home. Albert stops, and I take my hands down from covering my ears.

"I like those bad guys the best. Nice deep voices like mine. Come over to my eating ledge, Penny. Hummm...you need a boost." Albert lifts me up so I'm sitting on the edge of his rock shelf where the giant bowls of food steam.

"Um, Albert, what's in your...ah...meat sauce?" I have to ask him.

Albert smiles. "This is just some left-over odds and ends that I found last week. Mostly things lying squashed next to that human black mud river that isn't too far away."

"Black mud river? You mean the highway?" I think of the wildlife around this area. Antelope, rabbits, coyotes, and of course rattlesnakes. Any of which could be in this meat sauce. Albert clearly likes it. He eats his in a slurping frenzy.

"Penny! You haven't touched your spaghetti! Don't you want it?" Albert looks at my portion hungrily.

"Uh, help yourself Albert." I tell him quickly. "I actually ate not too long ago."

"OK." As I watch, Albert eats my share in two gulps.

"Now I'm ready to tell you the story of my life." Albert states after a satisfying burp. "Ooops. Pardon me. Mother always told me to gulp my food. And it always makes me burp."

Am I going to be critical? Albert is very big. He eats road kill. He loves opera. I need to be careful around this guy.

I pull out my tape recorder again to continue collecting the story of a lifetime. I have a deadline to meet. "OK, Albert. For the record." I address him in my most professional reporter manner.

Albert cleans up his kitchen as he talks. "Well, Penny, it all started about 65 million years ago. At least that's what Joe figures is how much time has gone by since I was out stomping the swamps around here. When there were swamps."

As Albert recounts fond memories, I jot down some notes and sketch in my field notebook. These are things I will check out later.

"What was your life like?" I ask, trying to picture this amazing prehistoric world.

"Well my family stayed together in a pack. Mother was the head of our clan because she was the strongest, the smartest and the nastiest." Albert smiles fondly. "All the other meat eaters were afraid of her."

I'm suddenly very glad that Albert's mom isn't standing in front of me. Then I remember from my science class that humans had maybe evolved from mammal-like creatures that were alive in dinosaur times. "Albert, do you remember any little furry guys running around? We humans might be related to them."

Albert is interested in this connection. "I don't remember anything furry that looked like you but there were some sneaky little 'saurs who would hang around underfoot and try to steal our food." Alberta shudders. "Or even eat our eggs! Can you imagine?"

"Like?" I prod.

"Well, there was these small guys, who thought they were really smart. They had big round eyes. Like this." Albert makes a circle with his two talons.

"Those might have been what we call *Stenonychosaurus*," I tell Albert.

Albert is not impressed. "That's a pretty big name for a bunch of puny smart tails. Then there were even shorter ones who ran so fast, even I could never catch one."

"Those might have been *Dromiceiomimus*."

Albert looks at me. "Really? I call them pests. They almost got my little sister, but she hatched just in time to bite one of them and scare it off. She was spunky—just like you, Penny." Albert looks at me fondly. Too fondly. "Yes. Those were the good old days. Everybody chasing somebody."

I frown. "Doesn't sound like the good old days to me."

Albert flexes his talons. "You had to be there. Anyway, this one beautiful day, there were only one or two fire mountains erupting, nothing serious, when a plump, wrinkly big leaf eater runs right past me. So, of course I had to chase it."

"Wait! Do you mean a dinosaur who ate wrinkly

big leaves or a dinosaur who is big and wrinkly?" A reporter has to have her facts straight.

"Wrinkly skin," Albert says, not at all upset at being stopped.

I remember Dad's description of Ms. Thoth. "I'll bet it was an *Edmontosaurus*. I've heard about them too."

"Right. Well, I almost had my teeth sunk in its big back end when one of those volcanoes starts spitting out some very nasty fire balls. It was every dinosaur for himself, so I headed to the nearest cover." Albert shudders at the memory.

As he talks, I sketch out a picture of a young Albert and an erupting volcano in my notebook, trying to capture that moment. "What happened next?"

Albert looks around his cave home. "I figured I'd hide in this cave until the eruption was over. But later, when I tried to leave, I found the entrance covered by rocks and grey soft stuff. I was sealed in here, tight as a plant eater's fat tummy. There was some funny air in the cave and it made me very sleepy. The next thing I know—"

Albert throws his small arms in the air "—I wake up 65 million years later and everything is changed! No trees. No swamps. No dinosaurs. I'm all alone." Albert starts sniffing again and big tears splash down on me. "Boo hooo hooo...it was terrible!"

"Take it easy Albert. Get a grip on yourself," I tell

him firmly. "You're soaking me." I rustle around in my trusty knapsack and pull out a bedsheet. "Here, you can use this to blow your nose." Albert blows, emitting a loud honking sound, and then dries his eyes.

"Thanks, Penny. You're very kind."

I look around at the cave and all its modern conveniences. "So then what happened?"

"Well, I was wandering around calling for my Mom when I almost stepped on Joe." Albert says beginning to smile again.

"Tell me about Joe," I ask, relieved that he has quit crying.

"Joe told me that he's one of the original people. I'd never heard of people before. There weren't any of you humans when we dinosaurs ran things. He's my Spirit Guide. We're friends. He helped me fix up my cave and he taught me how to speak human, which is actually pretty easy. You should try talking flying dinosaur...now that is tough." Albert proceeds to emit these awful screeches in what I presume is a language of some kind.

By now, Albert has licked his cooking pot completely clean and put it away on one of his rock shelves. I decide never to eat anything he cooks in those pots again. In fact, I will never eat anything he cooks, period.

"We call them *pterodactyls*, dinosaurs that fly...er...flew," I tell him.

Albert nods then goes on with his story. "Joe

called me a Thunder Being. He says that I kind of fit their legends about them."

Legends? "Joe must be a First Nations person—a North American Indian—from one of the nearby reserves." I tell Albert. "All around here used to be their land for thousands of years!"

Albert frowns. "Big deal. It used to be my land for millions of years. But now it's all changed and dried up and I'M LONELY!" he roars.

My ears are ringing. Here we go again. I try to comfort Albert before those big tears start up. I've heard of crocodile tears but this is my first experience with dinosaur tears. "There, there. You have friends now. You have Joe and now you have me."

Albert gives one more sniff into his bedsheet hanky. "Don't get me wrong, Penny. I appreciate that. But I have to know. What happened to my mother and all the other dinosaurs? Are they really ALL GONE?"

It's a good question. I check my watch. Yikes. Time is running out. Perry should have everything all ready for my live broadcast by now. I have to get back and quick!

"Albert, listen. I don't know for sure what happened to all the dinosaurs. I don't even know if there are any left, except for you. But I do know where we can find out all the answers."

Albert looks at me hopefully. "Really, Penny?"

I nod, quickly packing up my tape and notebook

but leaving Albert with the bedsheet. "I have to get back to my brother and my Dad or they will be worried. Can you show me the way?"

Albert nods reluctantly. "But I don't want you to leave."

"I have to go check some things out with my Dad. If it works out, we'll take you to a place where they know all about dinosaurs." I walk around Albert, studying him carefully. "But first...you need a disguise."

I look at him. He's at least five metres tall when he stands straight up and he weighs over a tonne. "I might have a few things in my knapsack that could work." But I suspect disguising Albert could be difficult even for me.

A short time later, standing in the afternoon sun outside the cave entrance, I look Albert over critically. He's now dressed in a fringed vest which is pretty tight but not too bad. It's one of Dad's old jackets, but I used my Swiss army knife to cut off the sleeves. It's a good thing Albert's arms are short. On his big head, he wears a cowboy hat somewhat the worse for wear after being crunched up in my knapsack from the last Calgary Stampede Rodeo Days.

"You need some kind of musical instrument." I dig around in my knapsack and I find my old tambourine. It's amazing what you throw in when you pack in a hurry. "I'll tie a long cord to this so you can wear it around your neck."

Albert likes the tambourine. It hangs right where

he can tap it with one of his talons. "Done! Now, listen, Albert—if anyone asks where you're from, you tell them...ah...um...you're a rock star from Russia, OK?"

Albert nods. "A rock star from Russia. Great. Now what?"

"Now we go and meet my Dad and my little brother and I put you on television. But we have to hurry."

I'm about to introduce a real, live dinosaur on my TV segment from the Badlands. I am going to be famous.

But I'm also going to have to convince my brother and my Dad that Albert is really just a lost Russian tourist who needs a ride to one of the most famous places in the world, the Royal Tyrrell Museum near Drumheller. I promised him I would help him find out what happened to all the dinosaurs. The dinosaur museum is where Albert will learn whether he is the last of his kind left on earth. But he probably won't like the answers. And a teenage *Albertosaurus* running around on a rampage while wearing a cowboy hat and carrying a tambourine is not a pretty picture.

"This could be tough," I think to myself, "even for Penny Moonstar!"

Chapter 8

"Penny! Where have you been? Everything's set up. Hurry up!" Perry looks hot and frazzled.

I've asked Albert to stay out of sight until I give him a signal. I'm still not sure how to introduce him to the world or my family. "Sorry, Perry. I, ah, I got a bit off track." I look over Perry's setup. It is pretty impressive. He has his computer set up on the hood of Dad's truck. A mic (that's what we TV types call a microphone, for short) and his mini-cam are attached to it. The mini-cam follows my movement as I get closer.

"OK, Penny, I've interfaced my computer with the satellite that feeds into the cable station. You should just beam right into the show in about ten seconds. Nine, eight, seven..."

I hold the small mic and smile into the camera as Perry counts down just like my floor director Scottie at the television studio at school.

"...three, two, you're on the air."

"Hey *Weird Science* fans! Penny 'For Your Thoughts' Moonstar coming at you, live from the Alberta Badlands! Because I'm on a remote, I can't actually answer questions unless you send them to the *CoolSchool* chat site." I look over at Perry. Will that work? He nods. I make a mental note to be nicer to my kid brother in future.

"Today I'm going to become famous and—" I catch myself. Instead of leading off with the big discovery, I give my viewers a little history about the Badlands, especially my favourites, the weather-sculpted rock hoodoos. Then I talk about the kind of creatures that live here, building up to the big moment.

"Now, I have a very special guest for you. I know this will be hard to believe...but..." I give the signal, waving my hands up in the air. Perry looks at me as if I've lost it.

Behind him I see Albert coming closer and closer. Boom. Boom. Shake. Boom. Boom. Shake. Perry looks down at the ground, frowning.

"For the first time, I'm going to introduce you to something only two human beings have ever seen alive before, here in the Badlands. Meet Albert O. Saurus, known to his friends as—Albert!"

Perry is leaning over his equipment, checking for

connections that might have shaken loose, when Albert taps him on the shoulder. "Hiya, kid." Perry looks up at Albert.

"Great hairy furballs, who are you?" Perry's voice squeaks.

I smile at Albert and hold the mic up in the general direction of his big head still wearing the cowboy hat. He smiles. This is our big moment. He leans down.

"Hi, my name is Albert and I'm a—" and then Perry's computer goes on a major burnout.

"—rock star from Russia," Albert finishes. Perry's computer is shooting sparks and his screen goes blank.

The commotion attracts Dad's attention. He comes running back.

"What the blazes is going on! Is the truck on fire?" Dad says as he sprays bottled water over the hood of his truck. "And who are you?" Dad stares at Albert.

"He's a—" I start.

"—rock star from Russia," Perry finishes. "Sorry, Dad. We were doing Penny's *CoolSchool* show."

Dad looks Albert over.

"Are you lost?"

Albert looks at me desperately.

"Yes he is," I jump in. "I found him wandering around out there, Dad. Can we help him? He needs to reconnect with his tour group."

"I can't imagine how a tour guide would forget someone of your unusual size," Dad comments, staring at Albert. Like most grown-ups, Dad sees what he expected to see: a tourist, not a dinosaur who should have been extinct 65 million years ago.

"Oh, I'm not as big as some of the others...from my group." Albert says quickly. "Really."

Dad shakes his head. "Must be quite the crowd. Where were you all headed?"

I jump in. "The Royal Tyrrell Museum, Dad. Maybe we could give him a ride there and he can find the others in his party?" Albert nods.

"Yeah, Dad." Perry pipes up. "Let's go to the Museum. We haven't been there since we were little kids."

Dad looks at all of us and rubs his chin. "Well, it is on our way to my next site. And I have a few friends who work there that I could check in with. But, you'd have to ride in the back of the truck, Albert. Is that OK with you?"

Albert raises the wrinkly ridge I think of as his eyebrows. "No problem, Albert." I tell him. "You'll enjoy it."

"Will it try to shake me off ?" he asks nervously.

"Ha ha, Albert," I laugh, and it sounds forced even to me. "You're such a joker. Although I'm sure it's much funnier in Russian."

I show Albert around the truck, open the door and point out the steering wheel, the buttons, the standard shift, knobs and things. I overhear Perry saying to Dad "I guess they don't have trucks like ours in Russia."

We help Albert climb into the back. He's heavy, but the truck has powerful rear end suspension and although it creaks and groans, it holds him. Then I hop in the cab with Perry and Dad. And we're off. Well not quite.

Dad tries to start the motor and the battery is dead. "What the... Perry! Did you use my truck battery to power your computer?" Dad looks at Perry, who looks guilty. Now I know how he managed enough power to do my live broadcast. Great. We are stuck in the Badlands with a truck that won't run.

"Can I help?" Albert asks from the back.

"Well...you do look like a very strong fellow." Dad looks over his shoulder at Albert in consideration. "Maybe if you can push the truck up to a certain speed we might be able to get it running and recharge the battery."

Albert has no trouble pushing the truck. The engine catches, Dad slows down and Albert gets back in. I hear the undercarriage scrape against the road for a second when Albert jumps on. But everything holds together and we're off to the Royal Tyrrell Museum.

"Too bad I didn't get to finish my TV segment," I quietly tell Perry. "Albert was going to let us in on a big secret."

"What? That's he's a one-man giant band?"

I make a mental note that sometimes my kid brother is a smart aleck but that doesn't mean I have to make a wisecrack in return. This story is bigger than both of us.

"No. Something really special," I patiently tell him, "but maybe it's a good thing that he didn't get to tell anyone."

"Tell what? What secret?" Perry asks me. Dad's looking so hard at the road I figure he is probably actually listening to our conversation. So I clam up.

I'm beginning to think that maybe it isn't safe for Albert to be exposed as who he really is. A lot of people might pay big time to find a real dinosaur, especially one as friendly as Albert. He wouldn't stand a chance in our world. Big game hunters might try to shoot and stuff him, scientists will want to subject him to all kinds of uncomfortable tests, and Hollywood would have him playing Godzilla in countless bad movie sequels until he would have to check into a hospital to get some peace and quiet. Then there's all those people who want their dinosaurs to be purple and fuzzy; they won't be big fans of Albert, even if he does sing opera.

Riding in the cozy family truck through the Badlands, I imagine that my brief transmission on *CoolSchool* has already made my fears come true. Maybe I said too much and someone out there has already figured it out. Did the mini-cam get a clear shot of Albert? It was a close-up of his face and he looks like an *Albertosaurus* mainly because he is one. What if my show was seen by the man with the creepy voice who called me earlier looking for Albert? Maybe my desire to be a big star has put my new friend in danger. Even the heat of the afternoon sun can't stop me from shivering.

Just then Dad starts complaining about the five

motorcyclists who are right behind us. "Pass me already!" Dad says, waving them by. He pulls over to the side and slows down, but the bikers stay behind us. I look through the back window. Albert is waving at them. He only has two talons on each hand so it looks like he's making the peace sign.

Maybe they don't appreciate that. Dad slows right down, and all the bikers finally zoom past. One of them has a camera and is snapping shots of Albert and us. He seems to be looking right at me. Then he makes a peace sign too and they all take off down the road.

"Weekend rebels," Dad snorts. "Everyone wants to be the next James Dean."

"Who's that, Dad?" Perry asks him. Dad just shakes his head.

As we drive towards the museum and a really good supper at a restaurant nearby, Perry asks me "So what kind of music does Albert like to play?"

"Opera," I tell him, "prehistoric opera."

"Neat." Perry looks back and waves at Albert who waves back. He's enjoying the view as we leave the Badlands and move into ranching country. "Maybe we'll get to hear him play sometime." Perry says to me. I seriously doubt it.

Albert taps on the window between the cab and the back of the truck. He points at the herds of different types of cattle we drive past, then to his mouth. He wants to jump out of the truck and grab one or two, but I shake my head. I hope we get to the restaurant soon. Thoughts of Albert chasing after herds of prized Black Angus, himself pursued by cowboys with rifles, are chilling.

"Dad, can we stop to eat soon?" I ask. "How about that hamburger place up ahead?"

"Yeah, hamburgers! Hey Dad, let's stop for a hamburger. We haven't had anything to eat since Mom's pork and beans!" Perry bounces up and down on the seat between Dad and me. Dad looks over at us and then back at Albert.

"I don't suppose he has any money to buy his own dinner, does he?"

"Uh, I doubt it, Dad. I think the tour group takes care of everything for visitors like him." Phew, this disguise business takes its toll on the brain.

Dad sighs as he turns the truck into a truck-stop hamburger place. "Well, I guess we can treat him this time in the name of international good will."

Albert kind of springs out of the back of the truck. "That was a fun ride, Penny. Are we there yet?"

I smile. "No, not yet. Have you ever had a hamburger, Albert?"

"No, I don't think so. Will it fill me up? I can eat a lot, you know."

Yikes, I think to myself. How many hamburgers can he eat? Maybe this wasn't such a good idea.

How many hamburgers can an adolescent *Albertosaurus* eat? We soon find out. His arms can't reach to hold things up to his mouth, so he arranges everything the way he likes it with his front talons, then he leans over and gulps things down. No one notices that he doesn't use a chair. He just looms over our table

Dad is basically speechless, though he makes some inarticulate gasping sounds. Other diners drift over to watch as Albert keeps eating. After about fifteen burgers, the waitress asks where Albert is from. I tell her he is a famous rock star from Russia, here on a tour.

She nods. "I didn't think he was from around here."

After twenty hamburgers, people start wondering how much he will eat. Truck drivers and motorcyclists bet each other as Albert carefully picks off the greens on each hamburger before swallowing it. The short order cook leaves the lettuce and tomato off after the twenty-fifth plate comes back to the kitchen with the garnish untouched.

Albert finally stops after downing fifty hamburgers loaded with onions, sauerkraut, cheese, bacon and mushrooms.

Then he chugs twelve extra-large vanilla milkshakes. The jumbo straws are too short and his mouth can't suck very well, but he manages.

Finally he sits back and burps. Then he smiles at the waitress and the crowd standing around us and says, "Thank you for the snack. It was delicious, except for the green and red stuff. I don't like those."

The audience starts clapping. Then a big guy with a thick red beard, wearing a black leather jacket with the words *Buffalo Bones Club* on his back, and carrying a motorcycle helmet, comes over and pounds Albert on the back as high up as he can reach. "That is the best thing I've ever seen, son. Want to join our bike group? We could use a monster like you."

Albert looks down at him politely. "Penny, what's a monster?"

How can I say this without hurting his feelings? "Ah, he means someone big and fierce-looking."

Perry, who is really impressed by the size of Albert's appetite and the crowd, has to open his big eight-year-old mouth and show how smart he is. "Albert, a monster is something big and ugly! Just...like...ah..." Luckily Perry shuts up at this moment because Albert is frowning and it's not a pleasant sight.

Everyone takes a step back except the biker, who bravely stands his ground. "Ugly? Me?" Albert shows his big shark teeth. Now even the biker backs away, but it could be Albert's onion-and-sauerkraut breath that makes him do it.

The motorcycle man shakes his head. "I meant it as a compliment, son. You should join up with us." Then he realizes what he is asking. "Of course, getting a bike big enough for you could be a problem. We'd have to get one custom-made."

Albert points to Dad, Perry and me. "I'm with them. Thank you. We're on our way to the Tyrrell Museum to join my tourist group."

The biker steps over to Dad who is looking a bit green because the waitress has just handed him the bill. "Here," the biker says gruffly as he thrusts a wad of money toward my Dad. "I bet those truckers that he would eat more than thirty burgers—and I won. Fifty must be some kind of world record. So I'm splitting my winnings with you."

The money is enough to pay for our supper with some left over. As we go out the restaurant's double doors, Albert has to duck down but he squeezes through OK, even though he is now fifty hamburgers and twelve milkshakes heavier.

The truck groans as Albert climbs into the back. As we leave the parking lot, everybody cheers and waves good-bye and I suspect they will remember Albert for a long, long time.

"Well, that was an experience." Dad says as we head down the highway. Just then Albert burps again.

"That will be the onions,"Perry says.

"I'm sure he ate an entire cow!" says Dad still in shock.

I dig Perry in the ribs. "That motorcycle man, the one in the restaurant. I saw him before."

Perry looks at me surprised. "When?"

I lower my voice. "He was one the bikers that passed us on the road, the one with the camera who took pictures of us."

Perry shrugs. "He was nice. He gave us some money and saved Dad from having a coronary."

Dad overhears that. "Who's having a coronary? If anyone does, it will be your friend, Albert. Fifty hamburgers. He's quite the meat-eater. Wait until I tell your Mother."

"Yeah, he is a real meat-eater," I mumble. Maybe Perry is right and seeing the motorcycle guy again is nothing to worry about. Hanging out with a real dinosaur is hard work and it's making me jumpy.

Just then, we see the direction sign for Bleriot's Ferry. It takes cars across the Red Deer River. The Tyrrell Museum is on the other side.

"ALBERT!" I yell back at him in the truck. "We're going to ride on a ferry! You'll love this!"

Turns out, Albert has a fear of deep running water. Actually, a fear of what lurks in the water. He stands nervously at the front of the ferry, then suddenly points at something floating by.

"There! See! That's one of them."

"One what?" I look into the water, but it's just a big stick drifting along.

Albert lowers his voice. "They're sneaky. You think they're not around, then CRUNCH...they grab you by the tail and try to drag you under! I know what I'm talking about. WATCH OUT." This time he is much louder.

I look at the old log that sweeps by us. "Albert, what are you talking about?"

Albert points at another log near the opposite shore. "I'm talking about those big, ugly, long things with teeth, that hide under the water."

Crocodilians? Is that what Albert is afraid of? Dad would know. Meanwhile Albert is making the other people on the ferry very nervous.

"Albert, there are no crocodiles around here anymore.

Those are just dead trees soaked with water so they float mostly under the surface. Trust me."

Albert remains unconvinced. He shakes his big head. "You'll see. When one of them makes splinters out of this flimsy boat thing, don't say I didn't warn you." Albert notices all the people staring at him. "All those other humans are afraid too. Look at them."

The nearby passengers are looking at Albert like he's crazy.

Just then Perry and Dad join us carrying cups of hot chocolate. Distracted from crocodiles for a moment, Albert reaches down for his jumbo cup. "Thank you, Perry," he says politely. "What is this? Looks like hot mud."

Perry looks at his hot chocolate. "Ha. Ha. Albert. Good joke. It tastes pretty good for mud!"

Albert carefully tries it. Likes it. And in one gulp it's gone. "Humm. Not bad. What kind of hot mud is it?"

Perry grins. "Chocolate mud."

Albert nods in appreciation. "Chocolate mud. Chocolate mud."

I ask Dad about the crocodiles during dinosaur times.

"They were giant crocodiles compared to today's varieties. And alligators too." Dad points out to the landscape around us as we near the opposite shore. "Things around here were very different when dinosaurs roamed these parts.

Dad continues, getting into one of his favourite topics. "There were swamps, water lilies, flowering plants, giant tall trees. And in the water, crocodiles

71

and alligators grabbing anything that got too close."

"See Penny. I told you so," says Albert. He listens carefully as Dad continues to describe all the terrors of giant crocodilians.

Meanwhile, Perry pulls me aside. "Hey, Big P. I saw that motorcycle guy again. The guy with the big red beard."

I look around in surprise. "Really? Where?"

"When we were getting our drinks. I saw him watching you and Albert. Then he made a call on his cell phone. When he saw me, he turned away. Maybe he's following us."

I think about it. "He could be a reporter in disguise!"

Perry looks at me. "What would he be reporting about? He was watching you guys. And he really wanted Albert to join their gang. Maybe he wants to recruit him." I shrug, pretending to be unconcerned, but it does seem strange.

Perry is really getting into it now. "Or he's a spy keeping an eye on Albert to make sure he returns to Russia."

Why did I say Albert was Russian? Couldn't I have said he was from Prince Edward Island or Ungava? Perry has seen too many bad Hollywood movies. "Perry, the Russians don't need to spy on their touring rock stars. Remember that Albert caused quite a stir at the restaurant eating so many hamburgers. Maybe it's a world record and the motorcyclist wants to enter it in the *Guinness Book of World Records*?"

Perry looks around, but the biker is not in sight. "I

think he was taking pictures of Albert too. But when he saw me watching him, he took off."

"It's probably nothing. Mind you, Albert is new to this country and we wouldn't want him hassled." I look around too. Nothing suspicious, except for people staring at a ten-foot-tall dinosaur disguised as a Russian rock star afraid of every little piece of wood that floats by.

Dad finishes his stories about the Cretaceous period. "OK everyone, time to get back in the truck. We're about to land on shore."

Albert is very happy to get on dry ground. "Will the Tyrrell Museum know if there are any dinosaurs left, Penny?" Albert asks me as he climbs into the back of the truck. "Maybe I should ask your Dad. He sure knows a lot. It was great hearing all about the good old days again."

"Albert, we don't want my Dad to know who you really are just yet. Or Perry, OK? Just our little secret for now."

"OK, Penny, if you say so."

As we drive down the highway, we see a sign for the Tyrrell Museum. It isn't far. Then Perry gives me a dig in the ribs. In the side mirror we can see the motorcycle man driving right behind us, and he's signaling to pass.

As he passes us again, I see him take pictures of Albert waving happily at him. Then he speeds ahead.

Dad frowns. "That's the guy who bet on Albert. Was he on the ferry too? I didn't see him."

Perry looks at me and I look at him. I think about telling Perry that Albert is not a Russian tourist but a dinosaur who has been asleep for over 65 million years. Then I think about how Perry would probably tell all his friends, and broadcast it across the entire World Wide Web. After all, he's just a kid.

But I wish I could tell someone. The motorcycle man is starting to make me very nervous. I hope that he isn't heading to the museum too.

Just then Albert bellows out one of his favourite opera arias and plays along on his tambourine. Dad groans. He's not much of an opera fan either. "Now I'll try it in *Pterodactyl!*" Albert starts screeching over the sound of the truck.

Dad looks over at us. There is pain on his face. "Penny, I must admit, I will be very happy to drop your friend off with his tourist group. Any ideas how to find them...fast?"

I smile at Dad. "Oh I think they will probably all look just like him." Dad nods, relieved.

"When we get to the Tyrrell, we'll connect Albert with his friends, then I'll call your Mother and tell her what we've been up to. Too bad she's missing all the fun."

Some fun. You haven't lived until you hear an *Albertosaurus* playing a tambourine and belting out the dying words of an evil Count in an opera loosely translated into flying dinosaur screeches. I can't wait to get to the museum.

Chapter 9

The Royal Tyrrell Museum is really impressive. It's in the middle of the Red Deer River Badlands and you can see it from quite a distance away. It's one of the world's most famous places for collections, research and displays of dinosaurs and other fossils. Visitors come here from all over the world.

It is late afternoon. Dad wants to reconnect Albert with his tour group then take us for a quick look through the museum.

"Penny, Perry, keep your eyes open. Do you see anyone resembling Albert?" Dad asks as we walk from the parking lot toward the front entrance. There are busloads of students and tourists arriving and leaving.

As we approach, with Albert eagerly bouncing

along behind us, I do see something that resembles Albert. Or what Albert really is. In front of the museum is a life-sized statue of an adult *Albertosaurus* chasing something. I turn to tell Albert that it isn't real, but it's too late.

"MOTHER!" Albert charges towards the statue which is surrounded by people taking pictures. He runs right up to it and stops, confused. Then he pokes at it with one talon. "Mother?"

"It isn't alive, Albert," I tell him, glad that his cowboy hat is still covering his head. The resemblance between the statue and Albert is obvious especially to me. But to the people all around that don't expect to see a live dinosaur, he's just a big, odd-looking tourist. With a tail everyone is too polite to mention. Everyone but Perry of course.

"That statue looks just like Albert." Perry stares at the model and then over at Albert. "What kind of dinosaur is this?" Perry reads the plaque aloud, sounding out the most complicated words because he's only eight after all.

"*Albertosaurus* chasing its prey. *Albertosaurus*. Hummm." He has a funny look on his face, the look Perry gets when his brain is working overtime and he's about to have a big idea. "Albert O. Saurus. Wait a minute..."

I grab Perry and drag him aside. "I'll explain everything later, Perry. Right now we have to get Albert inside to talk to someone who knows all about dinosaurs."

Meanwhile Dad has been asking around trying to find Albert's tour group. He joins us and shrugs his shoulders. "No luck. Maybe we'll connect with them inside."

Dad counts the leftover money from his share of the bet made at the restaurant. "Well, I have enough here to treat all of us to a quick tour through the museum, including Albert. Follow me."

It isn't easy dragging Albert away from the statue that looks like his mom, but soon we're in the line-up into the museum.

It's times like this that it's neat to have a Dad who's a geologist and knows all about old fossils. He tells us how the Tyrell museum is really special because it is the first modern museum to be dedicated to palaeontology.(That means the study of fossil animals and plants.) He talks about how a lot of the Badlands are the bottom of an ancient sea. The ice age covered it over, but when the glaciers retreated they scraped off the rock so that now it was one of the best places in the world to find fossils from prehistoric times.

Dad even remembers how a seven-year-old boy from a nearby city out walking his dog discovered a *Mosasaur!*

"What's that, Dad?" Perry asks.

"A giant marine lizard." Dad tells us. "It looked something like a huge Komodo Dragon with flippers and it used to hunt in the sea that was once here."

Perry is suitably impressed. "Another boy your age found the tracks of a group of *Ornithomimids* not far from here too. Those are dinosaurs that look like ostriches, only they lived over 75 million years ago."

I remember following Albert's footprints that looked like giant ostrich tracks. Only I can't tell anyone about those. "How come none of these dinosaurs are ever discovered by girls?" I ask Dad.

"Some were," Dad tells us. "In fact, one of the first known dinosaur finds was discovered by an intrepid young lady in England called Mary Anning, during the Victorian times! And don't forget, Penny, that the best *Tyrannosaurus Rex* find to date was discovered by a woman paleontologist."

"You mean Sue?" That's the name of the *T. Rex* skeleton found in Montana only a few years ago.

"Exactly," says Dad. "Named after the woman who discovered her."

As Dad pays our way in, I suddenly realize that one of Sue's cousins is no longer standing in line with us. "Where's Albert?" I ask, alarmed. How could he disappear? He's over five metres long and three metres tall! Dad and Perry look around.

"Maybe he found his tour group?" Dad says hopefully.

"I don't think so, Dad. We have to find him before he gets into trouble."

Dad smiles. "Now what kind of trouble could Albert possibly get into?"

Perry and I look at each other. "Plenty!" we both say at the same time. It's pretty clear that my little brother thinks he has figured out who Albert really is.

"Well, Penny, Albert is a big boy and if he can travel all the way from Russia I'm sure he can look after himself here," Dad tells me. "Now over in that display is a particularly nice example of..."

At that instant a man with a face that looks like it was carved out of the Badlands sees my Dad and comes rushing over.

"Ben Moonstar! Why didn't you tell us you were coming? We've just got in some museum-quality ammonite samples with colours you wouldn't believe!"

He's wearing a badge, and I guess he's one of the paleontologists but I don't hear the rest because they're pounding each other on the back and walking towards a door marked 'Authorized Personnel Only'. This is our chance to find Albert, so Perry and I take off toward the public exhibits.

"PENNY! PERRY!" I hear Dad call from behind me.

"We'll meet you by the gift shop in one hour!" I yell back. He nods and follows his friend. Dad can't resist a new ammonite find. They are pretty fantastic, I must admit, but I have a living fossil that concerns me now.

I send Perry off toward the *Introducing Fossils* exhibit while I head off in the other direction toward *Early Plants*. Where could Albert be? Had something happened to him? I'm ducking around people in the narrow passage between exhibits when I suddenly run into something solid. "Oof." No, it isn't Albert. It's the motorcycle man! There is no doubt about that red beard.

"Hey little lady. Take it easy. Where are you running off to in such a hurry?" I look up at him. He is tall. Not as tall as Albert of course, but big for a person. His thick rusty-coloured beard hides most of his face but he has a bald head. His eyes are kind of small and squinshy-looking. He's wearing his leather jacket and he's smiling. He seems nice enough until he grabs my arm.

"I remember you. You bet on Albert," I blurt out. I notice that he has one dangly earring shaped like a tarantula. Ugh. I quickly look away from it.

"Albert. Right." The man nods. "The one who ate so many hamburgers. More than any one human could?" I look at him suspiciously. What does he mean by that? "Up to now," I say quickly.

"Yes. Up to now." He looks around. "So where is your...ah...big friend?" The man is still holding my arm and I try to shake him off.

"He's looking at the exhibits of course, and trying to find his tour group." I tell him. Why is he so interested in Albert?

The man towers over almost anyone in the crowd. "I've been looking for your friend Albert. Why don't

you tell me where he is, umm?" And he gives me a shake.

"Hey! Mister! Let go of my sister."

It's rhyming Perry to the rescue, and I have to admit that I'm very happy to see my little brother. He glares up at the big man who looks down at him, still hanging on to my arm. "Oho! If it isn't the other little Moonstar. The computer hacker whiz."

Perry and I look at each other. How does he know about Perry and his computer? And how does he know our names? Perry tells me, "I'm getting Dad."

But before Perry can take off, the man grabs him by the arm too and now he has both of us. He starts dragging us deeper into the museum and away from Dad and the Gift Shop.

"A little spider told me all about you, Perry," the motorcycle man says. "Come with me and I'll bring you to your friend Albert. I think I know where he will be."

Should I yell for help, or does this man really know where Albert is? I'm not too worried, as long as we find Albert. No matter how big this guy is, he's no match for an *Albertosaurus*, I am sure of that.

"Where are you taking us?" I demand.

"To see Lillian." The man replies, dragging us along. "Unless I miss my guess, your Albert should be visiting with her right about now!"

Chapter 10

Lillian is also an *Albertosaurus*. But she isn't alive.
She is in the display gallery on the lower floor. She
looks stuffed, and I don't mean with hamburgers. I
wonder if she could have been one of Albert's sisters.

The motorcycle man stands in front of the display.
"Her name is Lillian, just like my dear old Mom who
was also as mean as one of these dinosaurs. Isn't she
lovely? I know because I'm a bit of a fossil collector
myself." Perry and I look at each other. This guy is
definitely weird. "Look at that display," he tells us.
"Do you kids know how much work it took to fix up
dear old Lill so she could be seen in public?"

"Thanks for showing us Lillan, but Albert isn't here
and we have to go now." I try to pull my arm away
from his big hammy fist. He still doesn't let go. He

checks around the display area. The circulation in my arm is starting to cut off. I can't tell if he means to hold on so tight or if he doesn't know his own strength.

"Hummm, I was sure we'd find Albert here. But he'll show up sooner or later, won't he, kids? This is what he wants to see."

I look at Perry. He looks at me and wiggles his ears. He has an escape plan.

"Wow! Penny! Do you see that big BUG over there?" Perry suddenly yells at the top of his voice. "It's running right under that lady's feet. I think it's a giant DUNG beetle!"

"Yikes!" I yell too. "And there's more of them! Bugs! BUGS!" Like a herd of buffalo heading for a cliff, the tourists stampede for the exits, running in every direction toward the glowing red signs.

The motorcycle man tries to hang on to us, but I don't think he's too fond of giant dung beetles either. "Where are they? Where are they?" He's yelling and stomping his feet, and then a group of hyper school-children swarm around us, looking for the dung beetles to catch them. Dazed by the shrill noise and movement, the motorcycle man relaxes his grip for a split second.

Perry and I jerk away from him and into the milling crowd of kids, snatch souvenir caps off their heads and try to blend in until we reach their teacher at one of the back exits, next to a sign that says *Day Tours and Hikes*.

We stay with the group, going through the doors and out into the late afternoon sun, keeping an eye out in case the man is following us. The teacher is counting the group for the third time and still coming up with too many bodies when we finally spot Albert. He's up ahead with the tour guide.

"Hey Penny! Perry! Over here!" He waves one of his little talon hands at us. "They're with me," he tells the guide. Albert is beside himself with excitement. "We're going to where the dinosaurs are," he tells us. "They're in something called a Dig. I can't wait."

I suspect that Albert is not going to like what he will find at a dig, but staying with him is safer than meeting up with that motorcycle man again. Maybe we will finally learn what happened to all the rest of the dinosaurs and if there are any others still alive in the world.

As we follow Albert, I tell Perry that I was glad he turned up when he did. "That man was acting really strange. He knows too much about us."

Perry nods. "He's following us. Maybe Ms. Thoth sent him."

I hadn't thought of that. She would know who we are and about Perry getting caught for hacking into that T.T. website. But why would our science teacher have someone follow us? The website with the tarantula alarm, the motorcycle man with his spider earring, Ms. Thoth with her spider collection—could there be a connection? It was a mystery all right. One that I would try to solve after we got back home, safe and sound.

Outside the museum, we follow a winding path through some amazing scenery. We hear the guide talking about the early days of fossil collecting and the famous Bone Wars. That was when people from different countries were competing with each other for the best dinosaur finds. Instead of a Gold Rush, it was a Bone Rush. Finally Dinosaur Provincial Park was created to protect all the dinosaur fossils in that area. Most of the bones found there are now in the Tyrrell Museum.

I know that Dad has special permission to look for fossils, especially if they are just lying on the surface of the ground. When he finds anything he thinks is very important, he photographs it, marks it on a map and then reports it to the University or the nearest museum.

Albert, ambling along in front of us, is impatient. "Why does that lady keep talking about bones? I don't care about bones. I want to see some dinosaurs." I think about telling Albert the horrible truth, but don't have the heart. He will find out soon enough.

We are last in the line-up as we approach the dig. The rest of the school kids and teachers are gathered in a semi-circle around the excavation. A number of archaeologists are working on something but it's hard to see what it is until we move closer.

Albert is looking all around but he doesn't see any dinosaurs. "Where are they? Where's the digs for the dinosaurs?" he asks. A lady archaeologist hears Albert's booming voice, stands up and smiles at us.

"Hello everyone. Welcome to our latest excavation. We are working on something very exciting here. All this area is a graveyard for *hadrosaurs*, also known as duckbill dinosaurs. We know they were the favourite food for *Albertosaurus* because we've also found more than fifty of their teeth here too! Some of them as big as teeth found from a small *T. Rex!*"

Everybody is impressed. But I notice that Albert is being unusually silent. I sneak a peek. He looks pale, at least I think he looks pale. It's hard to tell when someone is normally a kind of greenish gold. "Are you OK? Albert?" I ask him quietly. The archeologist is telling us how, so far, over 350 fossils have been recovered from this quarry. How they map and document every single bone so that they can get a picture of how these dinosaurs lived and why they died here at this one spot.

"These are mainly young *hadrosaurs* found here," she says. "They would be teenagers if they were human."

"My friend," croaks Albert next to me. "This is what happened to my fat-lip friend I used to play with. He's now just a pile...of...bones!"

The archaeologist looks over at us concerned. "Sir, are you all right?"

Albert stands up to his full height. "Now we're in for it," I think, edging away from him.

"Where are all the real dinosaurs, the living dinosaurs?" he roars. But the young woman archaeologist just smiles. She's heard this question a thousand times before.

"That's a very good question," she answers. "There are many theories about what happened to all the dinosaurs. The favourite one at this time is that a large meteorite struck the earth and the resulting blast and after-effect killed off most of the dinosaurs. It would have happened quickly. First the plants, then the plant-eaters, and then the predators, all the way up the food chain."

Albert kind of slumps down. He shakes his big head. "I don't feel very well."

"It's probably the heat. Why don't you and your friends go and rest in that shade near the rocks over there," she tells us kindly. "That should help."

As Perry and I accompany Albert over to some shade, we hear her tell the other tourists, "...but some of the creatures from that period are still with us today." Albert stops dead, listening hopefully.

"For example, crocodiles and alligators are here. Turtles. And a number of respected archaeologists also believe that some dinosaurs evolved into birds! Isn't that wonderful?"

Albert shudders. "I knew there were crocodiles in that water!" he mutters.

As I try to reassure Albert, Perry pulls me away. "OK, Big P. Albert is acting very strange. Why does he care so much about what happened to the dinosaurs? Unless he's... really...a dino...?"

"Distant...relative. He's a very, very, distant relative of dinosaurs. That's why he looks like one." I improvise quickly, since Albert remains in shock.

Perry looks at us skeptically. "Are you trying to tell me that there are still dinosaurs in Russia?"

"Nooo, not exactly. But they may have survived longer in Russia...and evolved into..."

Perry folds his arms. "...Into Russian rock stars? Give me a break, Pentacrinus!"

"Look, Peregrine," I try to bluff, "we know that mammoths lasted longer in Russia. Why not dinosaurs?"

Perry thinks this over. It sounds somewhat reasonable. It's a good thing he's only eight. But I know he's still suspicious.

"Come on Perry, how would you feel if you accidentally visited a mass graveyard of all your relatives? That's what just happened to Albert here." Perry looks at Albert a bit more sympathetically. He does look very depressed.

Perry goes over and pats Albert as high as he can reach. "Hey, Albert. Don't worry. They probably didn't feel a thing. Once that meteor hit, it would have been over in a *flash*."

I wince. "Perry, I hope that horrible pun was an accident."

Albert looks at us and what I dread begins to happen. Big tears fill his eyes. "Penny! They're all gone. The dinosaurs are gone! Now what will I do? Boo hoo hoo."

"There, see what you did?" I tell Perry grimly, as I dig through my knapsack for the bedsheet hanky. Then I remember I left it at Albert's cave.

"What? What?" said Perry. "Jumping furballs, it all happened over 65 million years ago. Big deal." Perry stalks off in a huff.

Now Albert really starts crying. "Everyone's gone. I'm all alone. No Mother, or brothers or sisters. No fat-lips to play with or eat. I wish I was dead too."

I stomp over to him with my hands on my hips. "Albert! Don't say that and don't even think it. What about your good friend, Joe? What about me? And Perry? Aren't we your friends? Don't we care about you?"

Albert stops crying. "Sniff. I guess so."

I pat him on his leg. "Besides, we can't be sure that you're the only dinosaur left. There are rumours about other dinosaurs, you know...."

"There are?" Albert looks at me hopefully.

"Yep!" I nod. "There's Nessie. She's supposed to be somewhere in Scotland. And there's the Ogopogo monster...ah...I mean...creature spotted off the Canadian west coast...and lots of other sightings too! So don't give up hope. We'll just keep searching. OK?"

Albert starts to look better. "OK, Penny."

"Good. Now I think that maybe we should rejoin our tour, OK? Maybe we can learn something useful to help us." Albert nods. But when I look for the others, everyone is gone. Even the archaeologists have quit. I wonder what time it is. The sun is setting, not a good sign. "Dad will be having a fit by now. Albert, let's get back to the museum." I look around again. "Hey, where's Perry?" Perry is gone too.

It is getting dark and Albert and I are next to a 65-million-year-old dinosaur cemetery. Then I hear something ominous. It's a deep rumbling sound.

"Albert, is that your stomach growling?" I ask him hopefully.

"No, Penny," he says. "It's coming from over there," and he points down the path where we walked up.

I'm getting a very bad feeling.

Chapter 11

"Take your hands off me!" It's Perry and the motorcycle man has him! Even worse, this time Red Beard's not alone. With him there are three other big guys wearing *Buffalo Bones Club* jackets. They're riding big black bikes and heading in our direction. Red Beard is holding a struggling Perry. Then I see that the other three guys are carrying something between them. It looks like...it's a big...net!

Albert and I are trapped by the rocks behind us. All four men stop in a semi-circle. Then they get off their bikes and come slowly toward us. Perry is trying to get away but its pretty hard when you're hanging up in the air. He gets in a couple of good kicks, though.

"Ouch...you little brat! Try that again and I'll throw you into that boneyard dig for the night." Perry stops kicking and gives me a guilty look.

"Sorry, Big P. They caught me further down the path. I was going to get Dad."

I'm standing protectively in front of Albert. I feel him swinging up to his full height. "Let go of my brother, you big bald-headed *STEGOCERAS!*" I yell at the motorcycle man. This is a dinosaur known for its thick skull and small brain.

"You mean this little dung beetle here?" he smirks, shaking Perry some more. "We're not going to hurt you two. Just step aside; it's that big guy we're after."

The other three men shake out the net. It looks strong, but they look uncertain. Albert is well over twice their height when he stands upright.

"He's a big one, Boss," one of the guys says nervously.

The Boss barks out. "Just throw the net over him. Four of us can hold him until the truck gets here."

"Albert!" I yell. "Run! Don't worry about us. It's you they want. Run!"

Albert leans over and picks me up. He puts me up on top of the rocks. "Don't worry Penny. I'm not running anywhere."

Then he roars. I feel the rocks shake under me.

The men hold their ground, but I can see some of them go pale. "Now you're in for it, you big...furballs!" Perry yells as he kicks at the motorcycle man.

"Drop my friend Perry now," Albert says to him, "and I won't make meat sauce out of you." And he roars again. Showing all of his very, very large sharp teeth.

"Get that net up! Throw it over him, you big

idiots!" Tarantula Earring yells, then he dumps Perry and runs over to help them try to capture Albert.

Perry rubs his arm. "Ooow." That does it. Albert has had enough.

"No more Mr. nice guy!" Albert roars and charges all four of them.

For a very big guy, he's fast. They throw the net up and Albert runs into it. He barely notices as he swings around. Four grown men are flung around as they try to hold on. Two crash into the sandstone rocks and slump down rubbing their sore heads. Two to go.

"ALBERT!" I scream at him. "Don't eat them— they'll make you sick!"

This really scares one of the guys still hanging on to the net. He suddenly lets go. "Sorry boss...another time." He grabs his bike and takes off. I hear his motorcycle fade into the distance.

The other two, bashed up from hitting the rocks, stagger off and soon they're gone too. But their boss is no coward. He shakes his fist at their backs as they take off. "You three losers are out of the Buffalo Bones Club," he yells at them.

Now it's Albert against the motorcycle man. Albert stands there draped in the net. Slowly he takes one of his talons and runs it down through the meshes. It's razor sharp and the net parts like butter. Then Albert smiles. It's not an encouraging sight.

"Albert, look, I'm just the messenger." Motorcycle Man starts sweating.

Albert takes one big step forward. Tarantula Earring takes one step back. "I was hired to capture you. We know who you really are...and my employer just wanted to meet you...honest...just chat with you about dinosaurs and life back then...that's all. We weren't going to hurt anyone. Especially—" and then he makes his mistake. "—especially those two little Moonstar brats!" He gives us a dirty look.

Albert roars again and charges.

"Albert! Don't kill him! There're laws against that now!" I yell.

Albert swings what's left of the net over the motorcycle man and drags him bouncing over rocks to the dig. Then he dumps him in, all wrapped up, right next to some of the duckbill skulls.

"Help! Help! You kids have to help me. You can't leave me here...it's getting dark!"

Albert lifts me down from the rocks and gently picks up Perry. We walk over to the edge of the excavation and look down. The man looks up at us hopefully. "Come on kids, have a heart. I can't stay out here all night. There's snakes and things out here."

"You're the biggest snake out here." I tell him. "Anyway, we brats have to go now."

"Bye," says Perry.

As we turn to head back to the museum, we see Dad marching toward us with the tour guide, fuming. "There you are!" he thunders. "Do you realize it's closing time? I was worried about you. We thought you were both lost."

Chapter 12

We see the flashing lights coming from a long way away. The RCMP cruiser looks out of place in the Badlands, almost like a space ship with all those whirring lights.

The car pulls into the parking lot, right beside our truck, and the officer gets out and spends a few minutes talking to Dad. Perry and I give Albert's rock star disguise a quick touch-up.

The Mountie comes toward us, walking slowly and thoughtfully.

"Shouldn't he be riding a horse?" Perry asks.

"Shhh. We have to be really grown-up and tell him everything." Well, almost everything.

"Hey, kids." I like the way his eyes twinkle, and he's wearing a really cool turban. "I understand you had an exciting day at the museum?"

The three of us nod.

"Your father says you were hassled by some strange men. One of them is tied up in a dino dig? Do you want to tell me all about it?"

"Uhhh, sure. It was Albert they were after." I say, feeling like a little kid. All of a sudden the day feels like it has been years long, and I'm very tired.

It seems like ages before they come down the hill: two security guards, the Mountie, and our suspected dino-kidnapper. The look he gives us is not nice, and I am glad he is wearing handcuffs.

When the motorcycle man is safely locked inside the cruiser, the Mountie talks to my Dad, and then he gets back in the car. They drive off into the dusk with the lights flashing.

"What will happen to that man?" Perry asks as we drive into the night, following the curving path of the cruiser's red taillights.

"He'll be charged with attempted kidnapping," Dad said.

We ride in companionable silence until Albert starts singing opera again. "Are we stuck with this guy forever?" Dad asks. "And what was that scene back at the museum?"

I'm too tired to come up with anything brilliant, so I embroider an old theme. "Albert's a rock star, and it happens all the time. His fans all want a piece of him."

Perry groans.

"What happened to his tour? We don't have to find him a place to stay, do we? I like Albert, mind you, but he seems to have a very limited selection of songs for a Russian rock star."

"Can he live with us, Dad? Can he?" Perry bounces up and down in excitement. "Albert can live with me in the basement."

"No." said Dad. "He can't. Absolutely no way. And that's final."

"It's OK, Dad." I tell him. "Albert has a friend called Joe Wolf Tail who lives nearby. I think Albert's going to become part of a cultural exchange program with his family."

"Good." Dad is relieved. He likes Albert, but not living in our house. "Uh, Dad?" I ask one last little favour. "Dad, can we drop him off there?"

"Where?" Dad is anxious to drop Albert off anywhere.

"Back where we found him."

The truck stops, Dad signals a turn, and we're headed back toward Albert's place.

As the moon to rises and the coyotes begin howling in the silver and black landscape, Albert imitates their yipping and soon we are all yipping and howling as the Moonstar truck heads back towards Albert's cave.

I'm happy because I will be able to visit with him one more time before we go home.

We take another route back so we don't have to use the Bleriot Ferry, which doesn't run at night anyway. Everything has worked out well, except for my interrupted *Weird Science* transmission. As I'm dozing off in the truck, lulled by the hum of the engine and Albert's rhythmic thumping of the tambourine, I keep hearing the voice of the motorcycle man: "My boss wants to meet him... My boss..." and I fall asleep.

Albert doesn't let me sleep for long, so I teach him another song. Soon even Dad is joining in. It's perfect for the occasion.

"The head bone's connected to the neck bone. The neck bone's connected to the backbone, the backbone's connected to the hip bone. Now hear the story of a dinosaur! Dem bones, dem bones, dem dry bones. Dem bones, dem bones, dem dry bones..." and so on into the night.

Later, while we are setting up the tent by the light of the truck headlights, Albert sneaks away into the dark to his cave. It was a tough day for Albert, seeing all those dinosaur bones and almost getting dinonapped. Dad and Perry are a bit worried about him wandering around in the Badlands in the dark, but I reassure them that Albert remembers the way back to his new home with Joe Wolf Tail.

Dad is tired from all that driving and soon falls asleep. Then, Perry kicks me with the foot of his sleeping bag. "Ouch. Quit that." I tell him.

"OK, Penny," he whispers so he won't wake up Dad. "Are you going to tell me who Albert really is? I know he's no Russian rock star. He doesn't know any rock songs, just opera stuff."

"You're too smart for me, little brother," I tell him, yawning. "OK. I'll tell you...but you have to keep it a secret."

"You can trust me," says Perry. And I know he's already thinking about which friends he's going to impress with the news.

"Albert is really..."

"Yes?" asks Perry eagerly.

I take a deep breath. "Albert is really a professional basketball player from the Yukon."

"What?"

"Yes. Because of the short summers there, people don't normally grow as big as him, so it's always been a problem to find good opponents to play with. That's why he's here. He's looking for other...basketball players who are as big as him...to compete against."

"You're kidding," Perry whispers. "A professional basketball player. Wow."

"Thanks for being such a brave kid back there," I tell him.

"You were pretty cool yourself, Big P," he replies, yawning.

"Goodnight, Perry."

"'Night, Penny."

"'Maybe those motorcycle guys were scouts for the *Harlem Globetrotters* and they just wanted to recruit Albert..." Perry is almost asleep.

"Maybe, Perry, but somehow I doubt it." I yawn. "They were playing with the wrong kind of net." Sometimes it's nice to have a younger brother, I think as I drift off myself.

Chapter 13

In the morning after breakfast, I tell Dad and Perry I have to find some *Weird Science* stories for the following week since 'Live from the Badlands' didn't go all that well. I take my recorder and wander away from our camp. I miss Albert already.

It is Perry's turn to do the dishes which is always a bit complicated when you're out camping and water is only for drinking. Dad is demonstrating how to use sand to scrub pans when I hear something from a nearby hoodoo.

"Psst. Penny. Over here!" It's Albert peeking out and I remember the first time I saw him doing the very same thing. I'm glad to see him, but I don't want to explain his presence to Dad and Perry a second time, so I quietly go over to join him.

"Penny! There's something I have to show you!"
"What?"

"It's a surprise. At my cave. Come on."

I can't resist, especially since Albert lets me ride on his tail, which is some kind of experience. We get to his cave very quickly, with me barely hanging on. It's interesting how when a dinosaur runs, their tail acts like a counter balance and it doesn't really move up and down that much, more side to side. It's like trying to stay on a mechanical bull, which I tried once during the Calgary Stampede.

Albert takes me to his cave. "Come and see my surprise. Joe brought it and set it up and everything. He even left a note."

I look around. On a stone ledge table not far from the hot pool sits a....can it be? I move closer.

"Albert. This looks like a state-of-the-art computer."

"A computer?" Albert asks. "What's it do?"

"Remember when I was interviewing you? Perry was using his computer and it did a major burnout because there wasn't enough power in Dad's truck battery to broadcast to the satellite."

Albert hands me a note. "Joe left this. It's pretty short. Joe doesn't like to talk much."

I read Joe's note out loud. Albert is right. It is pretty short. " 'Oki (hello), Albert. Dropped this off. Enjoy. Joe.' "

The computer is pretty high up and I pull over

something to stand on. It's already running, so I move the mouse on the mouse pad and a message comes on the screen.

Hello Albert. You don't know me. But I know about you. This is a gift. I have designed a webzine site for you. Now there is somewhere for people to go who want to know all about dinosaurs and their world.
Ask Penny for help.

From a secret admirer.

"This is pretty spooky, Albert. Could Joe be your secret admirer?"

"He's not a secret, Penny." Albert shakes his big head.

"Maybe someone else guessed who you are from the museum? Or maybe this is from the person who hired the motorcycle men.... Maybe it's a trap and they know how to reach you, through Joe."

"I trust Joe. He's my Spirit Guide." Albert is poking one of his talons at the keyboard. "It seems OK to me, Penny. Look, here's the name of my new webzine, whatever that is."

I look at the colourful logo that has popped up. "*Dinosaur Soup*. Neat!"

Albert thinks about this for a moment. "Well it could have been *Dinosaur Stew* or maybe *Dinosaur*

Sauce...but *Dinosaur Soup* is still pretty good."

"Sure," I tell him. "It's like a mixture of anything to do with dinosaurs, see? A soup recipe of dinosaur facts and other stuff. You can stir together dinosaur jokes and information, and drawings and—"

"—and stories about the good old days, and share our adventures like at the Tyrrell!" Albert begins to see the possibilities. "But what is a webzine, Penny?"

Now we're on my territory. I explain to Albert how a webzine is like a magazine on the website.

"What's a *website* exactly?" he asks me next. I sigh. This could take a while and I have to get back to Dad and Perry before they miss me.

"A website allows you to connect with anyone in the world through a computer. Because it's electronic, no one needs to know where you live. And it can be in any language."

"Even Pterodactyl?" he asks me.

"Oh Albert, once you figure how to write down Pterodactyl, you could even use other dinosaur languages. But I have to get back now, so good luck publishing your new webzine. I'll look forward to reading the first edition of *Dinosaur Soup*."

As I get ready to head back to our camp, I can't help realizing that Albert is on his way to becoming famous on the web and I've lost my last chance for the scoop of a lifetime. I can never tell anyone about him in case they find out where he lives. No more

Pulitzer Prize. I'm just a small time kid reporter. "Just make sure you always keep your cave a secret, Albert," I warn him as I head to the entrance. I'm not sure if I'm jealous or sad or what, but I don't feel too good.

Albert starts to sniff. "Penny!" he says, big dinosaur tears welling up in his eyes. "I'll miss you! You're my best friend now!"

"What about Joe? Or your secret admirer?" I remind him, close to tears myself.

"Oh, they're OK," he sniffs again, "but Penny, you're a kid, like me. And you're spunky, just like my sister...was. We have great adventures together. You're brave and smart and...and the note says you're supposed to *help* me!"

I suspect that Albert is crying crocodile tears this time instead of the real thing, just to get his own way, but then he turns away, as if he doesn't want me to see him getting emotional, and that convinces me. I'm the same way when I really feel sad.

"Look Albert, Perry and I should be able to connect with you via the Internet from home, and I can always e-mail you."

Sniff. "What's *e-mail?*"

I try to explain e-mail to Albert but it's hard since he isn't even sure about regular mail. He's not exactly close to a mail box or post office.

So I decide to help him at least with his first few webzine issues. I might even be able to work some of the research into my *Weird Science* show.

"Maybe we could work together on ideas and things that you can publish in your webzine. Who knows, we might even find another dinosaur out there somewhere."

After all, Albert is now hooked into cyberspace. And why not another dinosaur somewhere? Stranger things have happened. Strange things are happening right now!

"Penny! There's something I realized about those dinosaur bones we saw at the museum."

I wonder what he's thinking. "It all happened a long time ago Albert."

"Not to me. Just seems like yesterday. But I realize that it's like an opera. A tragedy. Where everyone dies at the end, right? But they really live on because I'm here to sing about them."

I smile fondly at Albert. He had found a unique way to deal with the loss of his prehistoric world. Now he is ready to face new adventures in my world.

Someday I even hope to meet the mysterious Joe Wolf Tail. That will have to wait for another visit to the Badlands. My family is waiting. Still, I have to ask:

"Albert, were those crocodile tears you were shedding just to make me feel sorry for you?"

Albert is insulted. "Crocodile tears! I would never have anything to do with those big, ugly snout-nosed log-fakers."

"Oh, Albert," I have to laugh.

I'm still laughing when I get back to the campsite and find Perry trying to repair his computer, and Dad packing all his equipment into the back of the truck.

"Did you get your story, Pentacrinus?" Perry asks, as impatient to go home as he was to come out here in the first place.

"In fact I did, Peregrine," I answer cheerfully. Even though I can't tell anybody.

"All aboard, then," Dad says, and we scramble into the truck. "We should stop for lunch along the road. How d'you two feel about hamburgers again?"

Perry makes a face.

"I have a better idea, Dad," I say as the truck pulls away from the home of my newfound friend. "Why don't we find some fantastic Dinosaur Soup?"

"You're weird, Penny," comments my brother as we head back home.

ABOUT THE AUTHOR

GERRI COOK has wanted to write children's books since she published her first short story in the local newspaper while in Grade Six, and every year it has been her New Year's resolution to complete her first one....Instead, she ended up writing and producing for television for over twenty years. During that time, many of the children's TV series she developed and/or wrote won awards and sold to countries around the world. She and her husband Steve Moore have their own independent production company, producing family friendly television for Canada and the world. But some ideas are just meant to be books first, and so Gerri is excited that she has finally kept her resolution and started this series of the adventures of intrepid junior journalist Penny and her 10-foot-tall friend, Albert O. Saurus, "live from the Canadian Badlands". Penny and her friends are partially inspired by Gerri's sister and three brothers, her stepson, and her many nieces and nephews. Gerri and Steve live in St. Albert, Canada, with their dog Smokey.

ABOUT THE ILLUSTRATORS

Chao Yu was born in Shandong Province, China, which is also known for its famous dinosaurs. She and her husband Jue Wang met in China where they were both artists. Since 1985 Chao has been illustrating children's books in China and Canada. In 1989 she won the National Children's Books Illustration Award in China. Chao and Jue came to Canada in 1990 as visiting scholars to teach Chinese painting at the University of Alberta. They have two children, Elan, who advised her parents on the illustrations for this book, and Justin. They all live in Edmonton with their dog Hunter.

More adventures with Penny and Albert coming soon!

Where The Buffalo Jump

By Gerri Cook   Illustrated by Chao Yu and Jue Wang
ISBN: 1-895836-95-6   Price: $9.95

Albert O. Saurus's new webzine, Dinosaur Soup "everything you wanted
to know about dinosaurs and here's one to ask", is attracting a growing
number of fans. It also catches the attention of that nefarious rare animal
collector, Tarantula Tax. T.T. who plans to capture Albert dead or alive.

Meanwhile Albert's best friend, intrepid kid journalist Penny Moonstar,
investigates the strange case of a prehistoric bison who is threatening
tourists at world famous archaeological site, Head-Smashed-In Buffalo
Jump. Albert asks his friend Joseph Wolf Tail, a Blackfoot cowboy, for
help. Together, they confront a vengeful buffalo spirit, avoid the
clutches of TT and even get a special invitation to a Pow Wow.

Christmas In The Badlands

By Gerri Cook   Illustrated by Chao Yu and Jue Wang
ISBN: 1-895836-94-8   Price: $9.95

Albert O. Saurus is homesick, especially when he has to face his first
Canadian winter. Penny Moonstar tries to cheer him up by telling him
about North American Christmas traditions. Albert especially likes the
idea of having his own Christmas tree in his secret cave in the Badlands
though no modern trees match the ones he remembers from 65 million
years ago.

Meanwhile Penny's infamous cousin from England is a surprise guest
for the holidays. Demolition Derek, a thirteen year old animal rights
activist who's in trouble for paint bombing taxidermist shop windows,
is making life miserable for all of them. So Penny decides to introduce
him to a special friend of hers for a lesson in manners of the prehistoric kind. Has Derek betrayed Albert to the evil Tarantula Tax? Will
T.T. find the secret cave and have Albert for a Christmas present? Or
can Penny and her unusual family help Albert find a way to bring
Christmas to the Badlands?

*To put in your special advance order sign on to www.dinosaursoup.com
or write to Dinosaur Soup Books Ltd. c/o The Books Collective,
214-21, 10405 Jasper Avenue Edmonton, Alberta Canada T5J 3S2*